EOIN COLFER

THE WISH LIST

EOIN COLFER

THE WISH LIST

PUFFIN BOOKS

PUFFIN BOOKS

Published by the Penguin Group
Penguin Books Ltd, 80 Strand, London WC2R 0RL, England
Penguin Putnam Inc., 375 Hudson Street, New York, New York 10014, USA
Penguin Books Australia Ltd, 250 Camberwell Road, Camberwell, Victoria 3124, Australia
Penguin Books Canada Ltd, 10 Alcorn Avenue, Toronto, Ontario, Canada M4V 3B2
Penguin Books India (P) Ltd, 11 Community Centre, Panchsheel Park, New Delhi – 110 017, India
Penguin Books (NZ) Ltd, Cnr Rosedale and Airborne Roads, Albany, Auckland, New Zealand
Penguin Books (South Africa) (Pty) Ltd, 24 Sturdee Avenue, Rosebank 2196, South Africa

Penguin Books Ltd, Registered Offices: 80 Strand, London WC2R 0RL, England

www.penguin.com

First published by The O'Brien Press Ltd 2000
Published in Puffin Books 2002
2

Text copyright © Eoin Colfer, 2000

Set in Perpetua

Printed in England by Clays Ltd, St Ives plc

British Library Cataloguing in Publication Data
A CIP catalogue record for this book is available from the British Library

ISBN 0–670–91385–5

For Donal,
'The Lord of Love'

CONTENTS

Chapter 1:   Double Act   1

Chapter 2:   Dead as Doornails   14

Chapter 3:   Unhappy Endings   24

Chapter 4:   Unwelcome Visitors   33

Chapter 5:   Makeover   54

Chapter 6:   Kissy Sissy   72

Chapter 7:   Football Crazy   90

Chapter 8:   The Equalizer   105

Chapter 9:   The Sad Bit   124

Chapter 10:   Burst Ball   139

Chapter 11:   A Spare Wish   147

Chapter 12:   Double Revenge   159

Chapter 13:   From a Great Height   175

Chapter 14:   Here and Thereafter   196

CHAPTER 1: DOUBLE ACT

MEG and Belch were doing a job. Meg and Belch. Sounded like some sort of comedy double act. But it wasn't. There was nothing funny about breaking into a pensioner's flat.

Raptor was slobbering on Meg's boots.

'Do we really need the mutt?' she hissed, wiping her dripping boot in the flowerbed.

Belch turned away from the window. Piggy eyes glared out from under gelled spikes of hair.

'Listen, Finn,' he whispered. 'Raptor is no mutt. He is a pure breed, from a long line.'

Meg rolled her eyes.

Belch returned to window-jimmying, worming the blade of the screwdriver between the frame and the sill.

For the thousandth time, Meg Finn wondered what she was doing here. How had she sunk this far – skulking around the granny flats with a lowlife like Belch Brennan? Her reflection glared accusingly from the window pane. For a second she saw the ghost of her mother in that face. The same wide blue eyes, the same braided blonde hair, even the same frown wrinkles between her eyebrows. What would Mam think of this latest escapade? Meg's involuntary blush answered the question for her.

Something split in the window frame.

'We're in,' grunted Belch. 'Let's go.'

Raptor scrabbled up the wall into the dark interior. He was the point-dog, sent in to check for hostiles. His orders were simple. Bite everything. If it screamed, it was hostile.

The pit bull was not what you'd call a stealth canine and managed to barge into every stick of furniture on the ground floor.

'Why don't we just ring the bell?' groaned Meg.

'Oh stop your whining, Finn,' snorted Belch. 'Old Lowrie is deaf as a post anyway. You could set off fireworks in there and he wouldn't stop snoring.'

Belch hoisted his considerable bulk over the sill, exposing a drooping belly in the process. Meg shuddered. Disgusting.

Her partner's face appeared from the darkness.

'Are you coming, Finn?'

Meg paused. This was it. The line between bold and bad. The decision was hers.

'Well? You're not chickening out on me, are you?'

Meg bristled. 'I'm not afraid of anything, Belch Brennan!'

Belch chuckled nastily. 'Prove it.'

He was manipulating her, and she knew it. But Meg Finn could never resist a dare. Placing her palms on the ledge, she vaulted nimbly into the room.

'That's how to break and enter, you big clod,' she said primly.

That remark could cost her later. But even Belch wouldn't waste time wrestling when there was robbing to be done. Luckily, he had the memory span of a particularly thick goldfish, so with any luck he'd have forgotten all about the comment by the time they'd completed their mission.

The room was musty, with a medicinal smell. Meg recognized it from the night she'd spent on the couch outside her mother's hospital room. The odours made what she was doing seem all the more terrible. How *could* she? Steal from a helpless pensioner?

She could because she needed the money to run away. Escape from Franco once and for all. Get on the ferry to Fishguard and never come back.

Think about the ferry, she told herself. Think about escaping. Get the money any way you can.

There was old-man stuff all over the room. Tins of pills and tubs of Vicks. Worthless. Belch pocketed them anyway.

'They could be heart pills, Belch,' whispered Meg. 'Your man could have a fit when he realizes he's been robbed. That'd make you a murderer.'

Belch shrugged. 'So what? One less crusty in the world. Oh the pain of it. Anyway, I don't know what you're whining about. Seein' as you're an accessory and all.'

Meg opened her mouth to object, but couldn't. It *was* true. She was an accessory to whatever happened here tonight.

'So give up yer moaning and go through the dresser. This old coot's got cash somewhere. All crusties do. So's they can leave it to someone!'

Another gem of wisdom from Belch. Her hand hovered over the knob on an ancient dresser. Open it, she told herself. Open it and face the consequences. Her fingers trembled, rigid with fear and shame. Ancient photographs lined the shelves. Yellowed eyes accused her from behind smoky glass. It was no use. Meg Finn might be bold, but she wasn't bad.

Belch elbowed her out of the way.

'Chicken,' he muttered in disgust.

That was when the light came on. Old Lowrie McCall stood on the stairs, brandishing an ancient shotgun. Obviously not as deaf as Belch had thought.

'What are you two at?' he rasped, his voice gravelly with sleep. It was a dopey sort of question really. Two intruders. Middle of the night. Up to their elbows in his stuff. What did he think they were doing?

Lowrie cocked the antique gun with his thumb. 'Well? I asked you a question.'

Belch belched casually, hence the name. 'We're robbin' the place, crusty. What does it look like?'

The old man descended the stairs, frowning. 'Actually, tubby, that's exactly what it looks like. Now get your paws out of my dresser before I ventilate your spotty head.'

Meg blinked. This was like something on the telly. One of those American cop shows where everyone had ponytails. If they were going to follow the script, then Belch would do something stupid, and the old chap would be forced to shoot the pair of them.

That's not what happened at all. What happened was that Raptor recognized the enemy and aimed for a bare leg hanging from the hem of a dressing gown.

The pit bull opened its jaws until the tendons cracked and gnashed down on Lowrie McCall's calf. The old man howled lustily, battering the dog with the shotgun's wooden stock. But he might as well have been bashing a cement block. Once Raptor had a hold on something, he wouldn't relinquish it until Belch told him – or it was dead.

Meg danced around frantically. 'Tell him to let go, Belch! Tell him!'

'No hurry. He needs to be taught a lesson after pointing a gun at me.'

'Get Raptor off him, Belch!' Meg screamed, and she snatched the gun from between Lowrie McCall's fingers.

Belch blinked. The stupid girl was crying! Blubbering away like a little fairy. And she had the gun pointed at Raptor.

'Ah here now, Finn!' It was funny, really. Didn't she know anything about shotguns?

'Call him off! I'm warning you.'

Belch spoke slowly, as one would to a toddler. 'That's a shotgun, eejit. You shoot from there and you'll splatter the old coot as well.'

Meg wavered for a moment. 'I don't care. At least he'll die quick. I'm giving you to three, Brennan. Seeing as you can't count to five.'

Belch mulled it over. He wasn't used to thinking so fast.

'One …'

Would Meg really do it? Not likely. Too soft.

'Two …'

Then again, after what she'd done to her stepda Franco. And she *was* a girl. Who knew with women?

'Thr—'

'OK, OK!' Best not to risk it. There'd be plenty of time for revenge later. 'Raptor! Heel, boy.'

The dog snarled, reluctant to release its wriggling prize.

'I SAID, HEEL!'

Instantly cowed, the pit bull spat out the remains of Lowrie McCall's calf and trotted to its master's side.

Meg ran to Lowrie McCall. He was spasming weakly on the lino, blood pumping from his open wound. There was a pale gleam in the crimson. To her horror Meg realized that it was bone.

'What have we done?' she sobbed. 'What have we done?'

Belch was unaffected by the crisis. 'So, a wrinkly kicks the bucket a few days early. So what?'

Meg brushed the tears from her eyes. 'We have to call an ambulance, Belch! Right now!'

Belch shook his head. 'No can do, Finn. There's no turning back now.'

McCall's eyes were losing focus. 'Please,' he rasped.

Meg pointed the gun at Belch. 'Get out! Go on.'

'Forget it, Meg.'

'I'll take the blame. You just go!'

Belch snorted. 'Sure. Just tell the guards you bit his leg. They'll definitely believe that.'

It was true. Every guard in town knew Belch Brennan and his mutt. There was no way out of this one. For the first time in her life, Meg Finn wasn't going to be able to smartmouth her way out of trouble.

Then things got worse. Belch took advantage of his partner's consternation and snatched the gun. A yellow-toothed grin pasted itself across his features.

'Point a gun at me will you?'

Meg felt tears bubbling over her lids. 'He's bleeding bad, Belch. Dying, maybe!'

Belch shrugged. 'So what?' He raised his gaze to Meg. 'And now I've got you to deal with.'

'Belch! Call an —'

'My reputation is at stake. If any of the lads ever found out a girl pointed a gun at me and lived …'

Meg knew Belch. He was going to make a big speech like he thought hard men were supposed to. By the end of it, he'd be so worked up you wouldn't know what he'd do. Meg decided not to wait around long enough to find out. Without a word, she turned and flung herself through the still-open window.

Belch nodded at his eager pit bull. 'Hunt, boy. Run her down.'

Raptor licked his teeth and was off. His master took his time. There was no hurry now. No one ever escaped Raptor. He knelt beside the pale pensioner.

'Don't go anywhere, Lowrie. I'll be back in a minute.'

The old man didn't answer.

Meg had a plan when she made her bid for freedom. She would run to the first house with a light on, and hammer on the door. She knew now that she would rather face the police than let old Lowrie die. Meg made only one mistake. One fatal mistake. In all the confusion and darkness, she turned right instead of left. Left led into a central courtyard, overlooked by practically every one of the granny flats. Salvation. Right led into the maintenance area. The central aerial and gas tank. Dead end.

Raptor skidded around the corner. Invisible but for gleaming teeth and snorts of steam billowing from his nostrils. He stood his ground, blocking the alley back from the maintenance area.

'Shoo!' said Meg hopefully. 'Home, boy.'

If the dog could have chuckled derisively, he would have. There was no way the girl was getting past.

Belch's shadow fell across the confined space. 'You're a rubbish criminal, Finn. Running straight down a cul-de-sac.' The twin gun barrels poked from the shadows, like black eyes.

'Belch. For God's sake. Call an ambulance — it's not too late.'

''Fraid it is. For you, anyway.'

The curve of the gas tank was cold against Meg's back. The line of the weld rubbed along her spine. Nowhere to go. The gun barrels swivelled and aimed at her.

'Come on, Belch. This isn't funny.'

'I'm not laughing, Finn.'

It was true. He wasn't.

'You're not going to shoot me. So just give me the few punches and get it over with.'

Belch shrugged. 'I've no choice, really. It's all right for you. You're only a kid, but I'm sixteen. Responsible for my own actions. This'll mean prison. And I think you'd squeal.'

Just yesterday Meg would've said: You *think*, Belcher? Pull the other one. But not now. This was a different Belch. This was how he was in the dark.

'I won't squeal, Belch, sure I'm an accessory.'

'True. Still …'

Belch let the sentence hang. Meg knew the onus was on her to prove her loyalty. She had to say what he wanted to hear.

'Who cares?' she mumbled, the words grating like broken glass in her throat. 'Who cares if another wrinkly dies? Not me, that's for sure.'

Belch studied her face, looking for the lie. Apparently he found it.

'Sorry,' he said, cocking the shotgun. 'I don't believe you.'

Then came the big mistake. The one that made all others on this night of bungling seem like minor errors. It was the last Belch would ever make.

Meg was right, Belch didn't intend to shoot her, just scare her a bit. Due to his hooligan ways, Belch Brennan was familiar with shotguns and their scatter patterns. He was perfectly aware that firing at this range would probably ignite the gas tank, and blow them both to hell. But a little warning shot, over her head — that was a different matter. Belch pointed the barrels almost vertical and leaned on the trigger.

Meg saw it in his eyes. Saw exactly what he was going to do. Was he mad?

'No, Belch – don't!'

But it was too late. His finger was halfway through the motion. No time to change his mind. Not that Belch wanted to. His mouth was already grinning at the thought of Meg's expression.

The boom was tremendous, filling the confined space and pulsing through the alleyway. It rattled around Meg and Belch's heads, bursting their eardrums. But they didn't care, because by that time they were both dead.

One little pellet did it. One tiny ball-bearing with a nick on its curves. The nick acted like a fin, sending it spiralling off its intended course. It hissed downwards, superheating the air in a nanosecond. A new gas tank would have stopped it, and this one should have been replaced a decade ago. The rusted metal collapsed under the minuscule onslaught, allowing the white-hot sphere access to highly flammable gas – BOOM!

A blackened chunk of metal smashed into Meg Finn, knocking her soul clean out of her skin.

The first few moments as a spirit are very disconcerting. The mind still thinks everything is the way it used to be, and tries to force physics on to the spirit world. How can I be flying down a vast tunnel *and* looking at myself spread-eagled across a ruptured gas tank? Obviously impossible. Conclusion: I'm dreaming.

So, Meg Finn told herself, I'm dreaming. A nice dream, for a change. No stepfathers with axes, or big lumps of guards trying to stuff her into the back of a police van. She decided to relax and enjoy it.

The tunnel was so huge as to appear boundless. The illusion was shattered by rings of blue light that pulsated along its length like the heartbeat of some fantastic creature. Other dots floated in the slightly liquid air. Meg realized these motes were, in fact, people.

People floating in a tunnel? Hadn't she heard something about that before? Something about a tunnel and a light.

So, Meg Finn told herself: I'm dead. She waited for the revelation to have some tremendous impact on her. Nothing. No convulsions. No screaming or hitching sobs. It was as though the tunnel itself had anaesthetized her mind. Not that her life had been any great shakes in the first place. She was probably better off out of it. Maybe she'd even get to see Mam again. Although her mother was probably in heaven, and Meg doubted that she was headed that way.

Maybe she could con Saint Peter with the sociology thing. It wasn't my fault. Society is to blame, blah di blah di blah. Always worked in juvenile court. There wasn't a dry eye in the place when Meg milked the story of her Mam's accident. Heaven might be a harder nut to crack.

Someone was calling her name. Must be an angel sent to talk her down the celestial landing strip. Still though, a bit woofy for an angel. You imagined them playing harps, with voices as sweet as … well … angels. Whatever this was, it sounded like it was chewing on a potful of tarmacadam.

Meg turned slowly. She wasn't the only person floating

on this particular current. Someone, or something, was spinning along beside her. One minute it was a dog, the next a boy. Canine features bubbled under a human skin, poking through like computer effects. It was horrible. Grotesque. Yet strangely familiar.

'Belch?' said Meg uncertainly. 'Is that you?'

Her voice sounded strange. Like there were holes in it. The thing that had been Belch could only howl in Scoobeydoo fashion. But it was her partner all right, unmistakably so. And it looked like the gas tank had done a real job on the boy and his mutt. Belch and Raptor, all mixed up like they'd been dumped in a blender. Oddly enough, the new mix suited Belch. As though it had been inside him all the time.

'Belch? Get a grip, will you?'

The dog-boy could only stare in horror as his fingers morphed from stubby digits to pit-bull claws. Tears and slobber rolled down his face, dripping in large gobbets from a furry chin.

Oh no, thought Meg. First I get saddled with him on Earth, now I have to put up with him for all eternity!

'Meg! Help me.'

Belch was giving her the puppy eyes. Pathetic.

'Get stuffed, Belch! You tried to kill me!'

She blinked. Belch *had* killed her! He'd killed them all!

'Murderer!' shouted Meg.

The old Belch would have retaliated. But not the new thing. He just … *it* just whined pathetically.

'This is all your fault, Belch!' screamed Meg. 'I told you not to shoot! I told you!'

They hurtled around a bend. Up ahead the tunnel split in two. That didn't take a whole lot of figuring. Up and down.

Good and bad. Heaven and hell. Meg swallowed. This was it. Payback for all the cruelty she'd inflicted on the people of Newford.

The currents bore them along at a terrific speed. There was no friction. No winds whipping at their clothes or ballooning their cheeks. Just an increasing heat-blast from the lower branch of the tunnel. As they drew closer, Meg could make out cinder-blackened figures with pitchforks dislodging stragglers clinging to the wall. Hurrying them along on their way to hell.

This wasn't real. It couldn't be happening to her. Fourteen-year-olds didn't die; they went through a troublesome phase and grew out of it.

Meg could see details now. The red demon-eye glow of the tunnel creatures. The silvery glint of their prongs. The job satisfaction in their grins.

Belch whined in dumb terror, pinwheeling his arms in the heavy air, as if that could save him. Meg steeled herself.

The gate to hell loomed before them. It seemed as large as the sun, and almost as hot. Meg balled her fists. She wasn't going down easy.

Then her course changed. Just a nudge to starboard, but enough to steer her away from the lower passage. A relieved sigh exploded from her lungs. Purgatory, limbo, reincarnation – she didn't care. Anything was better than whatever waited at the end of the red tunnel.

The Belch-Raptor combo wasn't so lucky. In a second the fiery current had him and he was gone, spinning into the inferno.

Meg had no time to worry about the fate of her associate. Whatever power had been guiding her suddenly vanished, leaving her careering with the force of her own momentum.

The tunnel wall reared before her. It looked soft. Soft and blue. Please let it be soft …

No such luck. Meg smashed into a unforgiving surface with an Earth speed of four hundred miles per hour. Not that speed makes any actual difference on the spiritual plain where kinetics are out the window. That's not to say that it didn't hurt.

CHAPTER 2: DEAD AS DOORNAILS

THE Devil was not happy.

'Two,' he said, drumming filed nails on the desktop. 'I was expecting two today.'

Beelzebub shuffled nervously. 'There are two, Master … sort of. I have them … it … whatever … in pit nineteen.'

'Two *humans*!' hissed Satan, tiny lightning bolts sparking between his horns. 'Not one youth and his dog! How did a dog get in here, anyway?'

'They were … blended together. One heaven of an accident,' stammered his aide-de-camp, consulting a clipboard. 'The boy is a true disciple. Very impressive human cycle. Bullying, torturing animals, theft, murder. A rap sheet as long as your tail. And the dog, a real hound of Satan. Tetanus injection sales have risen by fifteen per cent in the first quarter.'

The Lord of Darkness was not impressed. 'He's a plodder.'

'The dog?'

'No, you cretin! The boy! Unimaginative, brutal.'

Beelzebub shrugged. 'Evil is evil, Master.'

Satan wagged a fine-boned finger. 'No, you see, that's where you're wrong. That's why you're a minion, and I am the undisputed Lord of the Underworld. You have no vision, Bub, no flair.'

Beelzebub's fangs quivered in his mouth. He hated being called Bub. There wasn't another being in the universe who would dare to use that condescending abbreviation ... well, perhaps just one – a certain saint named Peter.

'These impulse sinners have no staying power. Their life expectancy is too short for them to wreak any real havoc. One major sin and they're gone. No planning, you see. No thought of getting away with it.'

Beelzebub nodded dutifully, as though he didn't get treated to this lecture at least a dozen times a millennium.

'But you give me one creative sinner and he'll be spreading the gospel of misery for decades before anyone catches him. If ever.'

'True, Master. Very true.'

Satan's eyes narrowed. 'You wouldn't be patronizing me, would you, Bub?'

'No,' croaked a very nervous senior demon. 'Of course not, Master.'

'Glad to hear it. Because if I thought for one second that I didn't have your undivided attention, I might move you from that apartment overlooking the Plain of Fire, and into the Dung Pit.'

Beelzebub flicked a forked tongue over suddenly dry lips. Dung was all very well at work, but you had to switch off sometime.

'Honestly, Master. The new boy is exceptional. Especially in his new ... state. A bit rough around the edges, certainly. But I'm sure he'll make a fine spit turner.'

'Spit turner! We're up to our wings in spit turners. I need some arch demons, someone with a sense of humour.' The Devil smoothed his jet-black goatee. 'The other one. That girl I was planning to greet personally. Where is she?'

Beelzebub flicked a page on his clipboard. 'Actually ...'

'Don't tell me.'

'We had her all the way through the tunnel ...'

'You lost her.'

Beelzebub nodded miserably.

'The one soul I tell you to look out for and you lose her. I think you're getting a bit old for the job, Bub.'

'No, Master, no,' stammered hell's Number Two, well aware what happened to demons past their prime. 'The closed-circuit cameras are down and we have to rely on tunnel mites for information. You know how unreliable they are, especially if they've been chewing soul residue.'

Satan sighed. 'Excuses, Bub. That's all I'm hearing. Excuses. We have all the technology. Limbo surveillance, the ectonet. And here we are relying on the gibberings of some inebriated tunnel mites.'

'Myishi assures me the system will be back on-line shortly.'

Satan scowled. 'Do you know how much that techno-phile's soul cost me? A fortune. And he can't even fix a few monitors.'

'Soon, Master —'

'Now! I want that errant soul found. It could just be snagged on a stalactite in the tunnel. If it's up for grabs, I want it grabbed.'

'But, Master,' protested Beelzebub. 'A lawyers' convention bus goes over the Grand Canyon this afternoon. We're expecting a bit of a glut.'

Satan rose to his hooves. The tailored pinstripe he wore combusted in blue flame, exposing the red sinew beneath.

Always the theatrics, thought Beelzebub.

'I don't care about lawyers. Who's going to sue me? No one. I want that girl! Have you read her file? Did you see what she did to that stepfather of hers? Brilliant. Totally original.'

The Devil's tone became silky smooth. His most seductive. And dangerous.

'Find her for me, Bub. Find her and bring her here. I don't care if you have to send a retrieval squad into the tunnel. Get her …'

Beelzebub waited for the inevitable threat.

'Because if you don't, I'll be holding interviews for a recently vacated position.' He paused pointedly. 'Yours.'

Satan loped into a corner, and began tearing strips from the suspended carcass of a cow. The meeting was over.

Beelzebub barrelled down the pulsating corridor, vaporizing drone souls indiscriminately with his trident. Their final squealing sizzle didn't cheer him up like it used to. He hated it when the Master got in one of his obsessive moods. He had to have exactly *that* soul, and no other would do. And God help … Beelzebub blinked nervously … *Lucifer* help the demon who disappointed him. He quickened his pace. You shouldn't even think the G word in this building. Somehow the Master always knew.

What was so special about this particular soul anyway? Some Irish girl. Admittedly it had always a bit special when you nabbed someone from the 'Land of Saints and Scholars', but that golden age was long gone. These days there were as many Irish down here as there were in America.

Beelzebub hopped into a gloomy alcove, pulling a black

mobile phone from the folds of his silk kaftan. Lovely little thing. All shiny and impressive. Myishi had run him up a pair. Top secret. Not even the boss knew about them. Devious admittedly. But he was, after all, a demon.

There were no numbers on the phone pad. Just some function buttons. This was a private line. There was only one person he'd ever call. His warty finger hovered over the pad for a moment, then pressed. He had no option. The apartment was at stake. And getting good accommodation in this neighbourhood was sheer hell.

Saint Peter was not happy. If he was such a big-shot holy saint, how come he had to sit outside the gates all the time while the rest of them enjoyed the fruits of heaven? Why couldn't James ever take a turn? Or John? Or Judas, for that matter. If there was anyone that owed him a favour, it was Judas. There was a strong contingent of the opinion that the tax collector shouldn't be up here at all. And if it hadn't been for yours truly putting in a good word for him, he'd still be floating around purgatory with the rest of the don't-knows.

Peter heaved open the cover of his ledger. What he wouldn't give for a good mainframe. A powerful server with plenty of workstations. But you rarely got any computer buffs up at the Pearlies. Most of them came out at the other end of the tunnel, especially since Lucifer began offering his 'own your own soul after a century' deal. So he was still stuck with balancing the accounts manually.

The points system was complicated, developed over thousands of years. And, of course, new transgressions were added every year. Members of boy bands and mime artists were two recent categories with heavy loading.

The system was straightforward enough. Even if you had

enough plus points on your sheet to keep you out of hell, that didn't mean you were a shoo-in to heaven. There was purgatory, limbo or reincarnation as a lower life form. If it was a close call, you got an interview with the chief apostle. Everyone said he was a bit quick with the reject button. A million souls on the lower levels prayed for the day Peter got his marching orders.

High above Peter's head, the tunnel's mouth pulsated in an azure sky. It was a fantastic sight if you cared to look, but Peter barely spared it a glance.

A soul floated from the mouth and ascended gently to the floor of Peter's office. The saint ran his finger down the lists. Luigi Fabrizzi. Eighty-two. Natural causes.

'*Mi scusi*,' said the Italian.

'Behind the line, please,' muttered Peter automatically, jabbing his pen at the floor.

Mr Fabrizzi glanced downwards. Brass trapdoor hinges protruded from the marble tiling.

'You're cutting it pretty fine, Fabrizzi,' commented Peter, in flawless Italian. The gift of tongues, another little bonus from the boss. 'Good early life, but you've been a right old nettle the last ten years.'

The Italian shrugged. 'I am old. It's my prerogative.'

Peter leaned back. He loved Italians. 'Oh really. And where exactly does it say that in the Bible?'

'It's not in the good book. I feel it in my heart.'

Peter ground his back teeth. Who except an Italian would argue at the gates of heaven?

He totted up the points quickly. You'd be surprised how all the little misdemeanours added up.

'I don't know, Luigi. The whole Mafioso thing in the fifties. I'm afraid it's put you over the limit.'

Fabrizzi paled. 'You don't mean …?'

'I'm afraid I do,' said Peter, reaching covertly beneath the rim of his desk for the limbo button.

The Italian clasped his hands in prayer … and the phone rang.

Peter rolled his eyes. Beelzebub again. Couldn't that demon do anything on his own? He pressed the receive button.

'Yes.'

'It's me. Beelzebub,' came the hushed reply.

'You don't say.'

'A bit of a problem down here, *compadre*.'

'I thought you liked problems.'

'Not this kind. My job is on the line.'

'Oh,' said Peter. 'That is a problem.'

Even though the archangel and the demon came from different ends of the spectrum, theologically speaking, they had, over the past few centuries, established something of a rapport. Nothing major. No exchanging of trade secrets or anything like that. But both men realized the similarities between their jobs. They also realized the mutual benefits of keeping the Earthbound spirits from destroying the planet. After all, what would be the point of spirits without bodies? So they kept in touch. So far their little communiqués had averted several presidential assassinations and a world war. If Beelzebub were to be replaced the new Number Two might not be as accommodating.

'Ah … *mi scusi*, Santa Pietro?' said the suddenly polite Luigi.

Peter waved at him irritably. 'Oh, go on in. And no more gangster stuff.'

'*Si. Si.* No more gangster stuff.'

Luigi skipped towards paradise, his youth miraculously restoring itself with every step. Peter returned to his conversation.

'So, what's the problem, *Bub?*' He grinned down the phone line. His opposite number would be spitting fire, but he'd have to swallow it if he wanted a favour.

'The Master is looking for a soul.'

'What about that lawyers' convention?'

'No. A specific soul. I thought if you had her at the Pearlies, we might trade.'

'Out of the question. An innocent in Hades. Can't be done.'

'This is no innocent. We were expecting her down here today. I don't know how she escaped.'

'Hmm.' Peter finger-combed his white beard. 'Gimme the stats.'

'Aah. Meg Finn. Fourteen. Irish. Gas explosion.'

Peter flicked to the Fs. 'Finn. Finn. Here we are. Meg Finn. Nice little line in misdemeanours. Not a whole lot on the plus side. Just the one big deposit right here at the end. Hold on, I'll do a count.'

Peter ran his finger down the good and bad columns, totting up in his head. A frown creased his brow.

'Hmm. That can't be right.'

'What's the problem?'

'Hang on there a second, Bub. I'm going to e-mail this to your handset.'

Myishi had equipped the phones with scanners, fax and e-mail. Peter ran the receiver over the relevant page and hit Send. A few seconds later he heard his counterpart draw a sharp breath. 'Well, I'll be damned.'

Peter nearly laughed. 'You getting the same count as me?'

'Yes. Dead even. A balanced account. She saved herself at the last minute. I haven't seen one of these since …'

'Since that rock 'n' roll singer with the hair.'

'Exactly. And look at all the trouble he caused when he went back.'

Peter was silent for a moment. 'This is a touchy one, Bub. Wars get started over this kind of thing.'

'I know. A single soul becomes very important all of a sudden.'

'We have to leave it alone, Beelzebub. One loose cannon on the mortal plain is enough.'

'Of course,' said Beelzebub soothingly. 'It's out of our hands now. Just let the girl seal her own fate. No one is worth sending in a Soul Man for.'

'Hmm,' said Peter, entirely unhappy with Beelzebub's acquiescence. 'Just as long as we understand each other.'

'Perfectly,' hissed the demon, pressing the Terminate button.

Peter stuffed the mobile into his pocket. This wasn't over. That sneaky tone had crept into Bub's voice. He intended sending a demon to Earth, to reclaim the lost soul. A Soul Man. Peter was certain of it. Beelzebub was going to risk untold repercussions on the mortal plain for the sake of one Irish girl. Who was this Finn person? And why was she suddenly the most popular spirit in the cosmos?

Beelzebub stuck his nose out of the shadows. All clear. So, Finn got to go back. Well, it wouldn't be for long. He would make sure of that. Just long enough to add a few more points to her negative column. Then Lucifer would have his precious soul. And Beelzebub would hold on to his job until the next crisis.

So he had lied to Peter. Big deal. He was a demon, wasn't he? What did that white-suited goody-two-shoes expect?

CHAPTER 3: UNHAPPY ENDINGS

MEG didn't want to open her eyes. So long as she lay here hiding behind her lids, she could invent her own little story to explain recent events. That was it. She'd just lie here forever, and never even peek at what lay outside her head.

So: the pains all over her body were not the result of smashing into the walls of a celestial blue tunnel, they were from the gas tank. That explained why she was lying down too. Doubtless she was in hospital, grievously injured. But alive. And the hallucinations, they were probably brought on by the painkillers. She would have laughed, if her sides weren't wracked with shooting pains. Obvious, really. And it made a lot more sense than the other version of the story. I mean, dog-boys and giant tunnels?

Meg was so confident in her new theory that she decided to risk cracking open her eyelids. Her initial impression was blue. A lot of blue. Still, don't panic. You get blue in hospitals. A soothing colour.

Then a pair of disembodied, bloodshot eyes blinked in the azure panorama, bringing her hopes for a happy ending crashing down around her ears.

A set of sooty teeth appeared beneath the eyes.

'Never seen nothing like that,' said a phantom mouth.

Faced with something like that, lying-down-with-your-eyes-closed tactics suddenly seemed dubious at best. Meg scrambled to her feet, back-pedalling until she was flattened against the tunnel wall. Yep, that tunnel again. Looked like the hospital theory was up the spout.

'Spectral trail,' continued the mouth, oblivious to Meg's discomfort. 'Blue, red, purple. Wow wow weee.'

Features and limbs flickered into focus around the slab-like teeth. Some form of creature stood on the ledge overlooking the tunnel chasm. A diminutive humanoid. Its blue-tinged skin matching the walls exactly. Perfect camouflage.

'What are you?' croaked Meg.

'What am I, asks the girl,' snorted the creature. 'What am I? I be resident. You be intruder. No greeting? No felicitations? Just ignorance and bluntness.'

Meg considered her options. The thing was small enough, maybe she could hit it with a rock and make her escape along the ledge. But escape to where? To what?

The creature scratched a pointed chin. 'You must pardon Flit, young lady. Company never land. Float on by. Floaty, floaty, floaty.'

'Where am I?' asked Meg.

Flit threw his arms wide. 'Where? Tunnel, girl. The tunnel. Life … tunnel … afterlife.'

Meg sighed. Just as she'd feared. Dead then. 'And you are?'

'Man once,' sighed the creature. 'Bad man. So now mite. Tunnel scraper. Flit's penance. Girl look.'

Flit hauled a wicker basket from behind a kink in the wall. 'Soul residue. Clog tunnel.'

Meg peered inside. The basket was full of glowing stones.

Blue, of course. She could be imagining it, but she would have sworn the stones were singing.

Flit stroked the stones lovingly. 'Two hundred baskets. Then Pearlies.'

Meg nodded. It made sense, she supposed. Sort of a heavenly community service.

'So that's it, is it? I'm a ... mite ... am I?'

Flit found that hilarious. 'Girl? Mite? Oh, no, no, *negatori*. Girl one in a million billion. Purple spectral trail.'

'I don't ...'

Flit rapped Meg's forehead with his knuckles. 'Ears open, girl! Blue trail Pearlies. Red trail pit. Purple trail, half-half.'

Meg gazed into the vastness of the tunnel. The recently deceased were zooming past her refuge on the ledge. Some flew so close that she could see the disbelief in their eyes.

'What spectral trail? I don't see any ...'

Then Flit passed a blue hand before her eyes, and she saw it. Behind each soul, a fiery discharge. Crimson or sky blue. Those with red trails were plucked from the stream, and sent spinning into the pit. Meg stared at her own hands. Violet sparks were playing around the tips of her fingers.

'See, girl, see! Purple. Goodie and baddie. Even-stevens. Fifty-fifty.'

Meg was starting to get the gist. 'So what happens now?'

'No Pearlies. No pit. Back.'

'Back?'

The thing that had once been a man nodded. 'Back. Fix the bad things.'

'Bad things?'

'Girl stupid parrot,' said Flit angrily. 'Learn speak proper! Bad things done in body life. Back, back, floaty back. Mend. Then spectral trail lovely blue.'

Meg's ghostly heart quickened. 'I can go back? Be alive again?'

Flit cackled, slapping his hands in mirth. 'Alive? No. Ghost – booh! Help wronged one. Use soul residue.'

It wasn't easy keeping track of this conversation. Flit had been out of touch with humanity for so long that his vocabulary had been eroded to the bare essentials. As far as Meg could figure it, she had a choice. Either stay here on the ledge, or go back and try to patch things up with old Lowrie. Some choice. A gibbering creature or a … make that two gibbering creatures. How did you take back a sin, anyway? What was she supposed to do?

'Hurry, girl,' advised Flit. 'Time ticking on, ticky ticky ticky. Good wasting away.'

Meg stared at her aura. Tiny red shoots were striating the purple. She swallowed. Once her ghostly energy ran out, it was down below with Belch for her. She could feel the pit drawing her like the North Pole's pull on an iron filing. Wisps of her aura broke off and were whipped into the abyss, like fluff down a plughole.

'How do I get back?'

The blue creature shrugged. 'Flit not sure. Never happen before. Flit just hear from other mites.'

'Well, what did Flit hear?'

Flit pointed at the marbled wall. 'Go through.'

'I tried that,' said Meg, rubbing her head. 'Didn't work.'

Flit frowned. 'Not think wall. Think hole.'

This sounded a bit like surfer logic to Meg. 'You're sure about that?'

'Nope,' admitted the tunnel mite. 'Crank tell I.'

Crank? Probably another blue creature with limited vocabulary. Meg tried to marshal her brain into some sort of order. Hole, she thought. Hole hole hole. The notion gripped her mind and spiralled in on itself like a mini-twister. Soon the word boomed in her head, pounding with her pulse. Hole hole hole. What was going on here? She'd never been able to concentrate on one thing her entire life. Maybe that was it. Life wasn't here to distract her now.

She stretched out a hand. The wall did seem less solid now. Fluid somehow, as though it was a slow wave rippling with barely noticeable momentum. Her fingers brushed the surface and sank into it. Silver sparks danced around the contact point.

'See!' gloated the mite.

Meg whipped her hand back, flexing the fingers experimentally. Everything seemed in working order. Not bad for a dead girl.

'Go, girl – go!' urged Flit. 'Pit strong here.'

Meg nodded. The further away she was from that thing, the longer her spectral trail would last. And she'd need every ounce of strength in what was left of her body to make it up to old Lowrie.

'OK. I'm going. I just hope you're right. This'd better not be a short cut to hell.'

'No, no, no. Flit sure. Straight homey home.'

No point in hanging around here putting it off. Into the wall and be done with it. She'd never been afraid of anything in her life, and she wasn't going to start in her afterlife. She took a deep breath and …

'Girl, wait!'

'What?' spluttered a startled Meg.

'Here.'

Flit pressed something into her hand. Two small stones from his basket. Blue with silver ripples.

'Soul residue. Extra batteries.'

'Thanks, Flit,' said Meg, stuffing the stones deep into the pocket of her combats. That was all she needed. Some rocks. Still, better not dump them in front of the little guy. Might hurt his feelings.

'Girl go now! Fast. Road-Runner fast.'

'Beep beep,' said Meg nervously.

She reached into the rock face again. The sparks danced around her wrist, then her elbow, then she was gone.

Myishi was fiddling around in Belch's brain.

'Well?' said Beelzebub impatiently.

'Don't rush me,' muttered the diminutive oriental, not bothering to raise his eyes from the grey jelly before him.

'I'm on a tight schedule here, Myishi. Is he worth salvaging or not?'

Myishi straightened, shaking the slop from his fingers.

'Not in this state. Total burnout. The canine brain meld blew his mind. Literally.'

Sparks rippled at the end of Beelzebub's talons. 'Damn it to heaven! I need some background on that girl!'

The computer wizard grinned smugly. 'No problem, Beelzebub-san. I can uplink him.'

Computers were something of a mystery to hell's Number Two, a bit like transubstantiation.

'Uplink?'

Myishi grinned nastily. 'On Earth, my methods were somewhat curtailed by professional ethics. Here ...'

He didn't need to finish the sentence. In Hades, human rights were no longer an issue. Myishi removed a nasty looking object from his box of tricks. It resembled a small monitor on a metal stake. Without hesitation the programmer plunged it into the morass of Belch's brain.

Beelzebub winced. Myishi was one creepy individual. He made Doctor Frankenstein look like a boy scout.

'The brain spike. I love this little baby. The brain's own electrical impulses provide the power source. Ingenious, if I do say so myself.'

'Absolutely,' agreed Beelzebub, feeling just a tad faint.

Myishi pulled a remote from the pocket of his designer suit, smearing the silk with gobbets of brain matter.

'Now, let's see what this creature saw.'

The tiny screen flickered into life, and the two demons saw themselves staring at themselves as Belch saw them. It was all very confusing. The sort of thing that would give you a headache.

'That's no use, you moron.'

Myishi bit his bottom lip to hold in a reply. Beelzebub made a mental note. Watch him. Getting uppity.

'I'll rewind it.'

The picture wavered and sped into reverse. Belch flew down the tunnel, and was born again. Only in his mind of course.

'Right. Play.'

On the screen, Belch was once again grinning down at the writhing pensioner.

'I like this boy,' commented Myishi. 'Real talent.'

'Plodder,' sniffed Beelzebub, ever the hypocrite. 'OK, hold it there!'

Myishi jabbed at the controls and the memory playback froze. In the jittering frame, Meg Finn was kneeling protectively over the frame of the injured old man.

'Aha!' said Beelzebub. 'She protected him. That's what

got her off the hook. What are the odds of that? Must be a million to one.'

Myishi consulted a calculator the size of a credit card.

'Eighty-seven million to one, actually,' he corrected, the words plopping smarmily from between his lips.

Beelzebub counted to ten. You'd need the patience of a saint to put up with this smart alec. And he was no saint. He pointed his trident threateningly at the computer programmer.

'This blob is no good to me like this, and neither are you if you can't fix him up somehow.'

Myishi grinned, unfazed. 'No problem, Beelzebub-san. I'll install a virtual help hologram, and upgrade him from catatonic to … let's say … dogged, if you'll excuse the pun.'

'What about infernal?'

'Can't be done. Not with his cranium. Very few skulls can support true evil, takes real strength of character. This particular specimen is never going to be anything more than a thug.'

'Dogged will have to do, then.'

Myishi's manicured nails clicked on the remote pad. 'That added to the canine genes should turn him into a right automaton. Once you set him in motion, he won't stop until the job is done, or his life force runs out.'

Myishi hit Send, and Belch's frame spasmed as the bytes ran down the brain spike. 'What's all the urgency, anyway? What have you got in store for this guy?'

'This is my new Soul Man,' said Beelzebub, his eyes shining. 'He's going back to reclaim our lost spirit.'

Myishi stroked his goatee, a miniature version of the Devil's own. 'I'd better juice him up, then. A few CCs of liquefied residue straight into the cortex. He ... it'll be running smoother than a newborn babe.'

'It?' noted Beelzebub. 'You can't get the dog out of him?'

'No, Beelzebub-san. The mainframe is too corrupted.'

'Mainframe?' Beelzebub was certain Myishi used these technical terms only to confuse him. He was, of course, exactly right.

'Mainframe – brain. Imagine trying to unmix salt and water with a spoon.' All this was said in a tone of barely disguised condescension.

'How soon will he be ready?'

Myishi shrugged casually. 'A day, perhaps two.'

Beelzebub had had enough of all this flippancy. It was true he could not afford to nullify Myishi's soul, but he could certainly cause him some discomfort.

He allowed a sizeable charge to build up in his trident, and discharged it into Myishi's behind. The programmer executed a high jump that would not have shamed an Olympian.

'I need him in two hours. If I don't have him in two hours, there's a lot more where that came from.'

Myishi nodded, cheeks ballooning with swallowed screams.

Beelzebub smiled, his good humour restored. 'Good. I'm glad we understand each other.'

He turned to go, the folds of his black kaftan swirling around his ankles. 'Oh, and Myishi?'

'*Hai*, Beelzebub-san?'

'Put the top of his skull back on, there's a good fellow.'

CHAPTER 4: UNWELCOME VISITORS

LOWRIE McCall's leg was forecasting rain. Two years now since that hound had taken a chunk out of him, and the leg still wasn't right. Never would be either. The doctors said he'd walk with a limp for the rest of his life. Lowrie chuckled mirthlessly. The rest of his life? That was a laugh.

Lowrie lit up a fat, stinking cigar. He'd started smoking again. Why not? No one was around to complain, and the nicotine would never have a chance to kill him.

It hadn't always been like this. All doom and gloom. But now ... well, things were different now. He could trace it all back to that night, two years ago, lying on the floor with his life's blood pooling on the lino around him. It had hit him then that he was going to die. Maybe not then, but some-time. His interest in life just stopped. What was the point? Heaven? Balderdash. There was no justice above ground, so why should there be any under it? Why all the effort, then? What was the point in being good? Lowrie still hadn't answered that question. And, until he could, there didn't seem to be much point to anything.

Lowrie got fed up looking out the window, and decided

he'd chance a bit of telly. Afternoon television. The pastime of the past-it. After five minutes of elementary watercolour and cookery corner, he realized he wasn't that desperate just yet and switched the box off. The garden. He'd go pull a few weeds in the garden.

But of course his leg had been right, and the rain began to pelt down on the tiny square the council optimistically called a 'green area'. Lowrie sighed. Was anything going to go right ever again? Where was the wisecracking fine figure of a man that he used to be? Where had his life gone?

Lowrie had spent so much time mulling over these particular questions that he had managed to isolate a few key moments in his past. Ones where he had a choice to make, and made the wrong one. A litany of mistakes. A list of would haves, could haves and should haves. Not that there was any point in thinking about it. It wasn't as if he could change anything now. He put a hand over his ribcage, feeling the thump of his heart. Especially not now.

So, how to round out this rollercoaster of a day? Take some medicine perhaps. Go for a limp down to the newsagent's, or, oh the excitement, a card of bingo in the community centre.

Meg Finn hurtled out of the afterlife and into Lowrie McCall's armchair. And because she wasn't thinking HOLE any more, it was as solid to her as to you and me. The chair's springs wheezed in protest, brass casters sending it spinning across the floor.

Lowrie did not jerk backwards in shock. He jerked backwards because the careering chair flipped his cane from under him. He went down in a heap, grasping at the bookcase as he fell. Not a good move, really. The top-heavy shelving teetered past the correctable angle and crashed down on the old man.

A few moments of dazed confusion followed all around. Meg gazed dopily at the motes of dust spiralling upwards from the ancient cushion. Dust. Real dust. From the real world. She was back. Maybe she'd never been away. The chair was real enough. So, a possible theory: Belch's shotgun blast had blown her through old Lowrie's window, and the chair had broken her fall. Hmm. Dubious. Several holes in the reasoning. Still, though, no harder to believe than melting into a tunnel wall, purple spectral trails, verbally challenged mites and all the rest.

Lowrie finally managed to focus. 'You!' he gasped from under a pile of *National Geographic*s. 'Meg Finn!'

'Hmm?' said Meg distractedly.

'But you're dead. I saw the body!'

Ah well. Another theory up the spout.

'My body?'

'Yes. Not a pretty sight, I can tell you.'

Meg winced. She must have been in a bad way by the time they peeled her off that tank.

'How was my face?'

'Not much in the way of teeth.'

A couple of things occurred to Lowrie then. One, he was conducting a conversation with a dead person. Two, he couldn't breathe!

'How do I look now?' ventured Meg nervously.

'Eehhhhh,' wheezed Lowrie, his forehead turning pastel blue.

'That bad?'

The old man, with no more air for chit chat, jabbed a finger at the heavy bookshelf straddling his chest.

The penny dropped. Meg vaulted from the comfort of a real live chair and put her weight behind the bookcase. The heavy pine shelving lifted and spun like a beermat off a bar. It had cost Meg no more effort than tossing a coin. The case collided with the wall, tearing a right-angled rent in the plasterboard. What books there had been on its shelving fluttered to the ground like multi-winged moths.

'Wow,' said Meg, staring at her hands. They looked the same, not swollen like Popeye's or anything. But somehow she was ten times stronger.

Lowrie sucked in a whistling breath. 'Huff ... haa,' he coughed.

'You're welcome,' muttered Meg, flexing her fingers.

'I'm not ... aheh ... thanking you, you delinquent!'

Meg blinked. 'But I just ...'

Lowrie shook his fist from the floor. 'You just what? You just broke into my flat and had your dog take a chunk out of my leg!'

'That wasn't my —'

'Crippling me for whatever's left of my miserable life.'

'Ah here now. Don't let's get carried away.'

'Carried away?'

'At least you're not dead!' retorted Meg, feeling a bit sniffly. 'I wound up wrapped around your stupid gas tank.'

Lowrie paused. The girl was right. If she was a girl. If he wasn't dreaming all this. An hallucination brought on by oxygen deprivation. A bookcase across the lungs will do that to a person.

'What are you anyway? An angel?'

Meg snorted. 'Hardly. I'm a nothing. Between heaven and hell. An in-betweener. That's why I had to come back. To help the one I've sinned against, according to that blue-skinned gom.'

Lowrie was a bit lost at this stage. Blue-skinned goms and in-betweeners. What was the girl blathering on about? Who knew with young people? Between rap music and sticking earrings in their bellies, Lowrie could never fathom normal kids, never mind phantom ones. But something she said registered.

'So, there is a heaven?'

Meg shrugged. 'Apparently. Depending on your spectral trail. Red or blue. Or, in my case, purple.'

Another riddle. Or the ramblings of a lunatic. Who knew. Maybe his mind had conjured up this whole event. So he wouldn't feel so bad about … things.

'So, you have to help me?'

Meg squinted suspiciously. 'S'pose.'

Lowrie struggled up on one elbow. 'Well, you're too bloody late! You can't help me now! No one can.'

'You only got bitten on the leg. No big deal.'

The old man flapped around for his cane. 'Not that, you moron. That was two years ago!'

If Meg had had any red corpuscles they would have drained from her face in shock. Two years! She'd been gone that long? She'd be forgotten by now, with nothing to show she'd ever been here. Not even fond memories in the minds of those who'd known her.

'A delinquent ghost.' Lowrie's voice broke into her thoughts. 'That's all I need. Well, do something useful for once in your life, or afterlife, and help me up.'

Lowrie stretched out his hand. It was brown and twisted, with knuckles like conkers. Meg stared at the fingers reaching for her. She had to help. That was why she was here.

'Well, come on. It's your fault I can't get up on my own in the first place.'

Meg leaned over to help the pensioner. Their fingers touched, or rather didn't. The hands slid into each other with a flurry of translucent sparks. Before she knew what was going on, Lowrie's life force had sucked her in up to the elbow, then the waist.

'Let me go!' she screamed.

Lowrie's eyes were stretched in confusion. 'I'm not … it's not,' he stuttered.

The two beings flowed together, snapping into the same space. Meg was in Lowrie McCall, and he was wrapped around her.

It was eerie, disgusting, terrifying. Meg's spirit flowed to fill the available space. Her hands were conker-knuckled, her neck wobbled and her eyes were glazed and gritty.

'Let me out,' she screamed in her old man's voice, jumping to her feet – old-man feet with chronic fallen arches. But the body had her like a wetsuit, invading every ghostly nerve ending. Meg could see the liver spots on her hands, and the yellowed Aran sweater drooping in folds from her arms, and wiry hair from bushy eyebrows drooping into her line of vision.

'Help!' she wheezed, the shock gripping Lowrie's windpipe like a clamp. 'Help me!'

So Meg Finn ran. She sprinted through the granny flat, hopping herself off walls in an attempt to escape the decrepit body. But it was no use. They were locked together like spliced rope.

Lowrie McCall was in there too, not in control any more, but aware, watching the walls fly past, as though there wasn't a hunk of scar tissue in his calf. Feeling his heart thumping in his chest. Thumping but not racing! He was young again, with the energy and enthusiasm of youth. Lowrie wanted to laugh, but he couldn't. His mouth wasn't his any more, not to control. It was as though he was sitting in a one-seat cinema, watching his life flash by on the silver screen.

Lowrie may have liked being rejuvenated, but Meg certainly did not appreciate having her spirit encased in the sagging flesh of an old man. She burst through the front door and on to the cracked and graffitied path. The cold rain bounced off her now balding scalp. The water saturated the Aran sweater, stretching it down around her knees like a woolly water ring. The Lowrie-Meg thing skidded around corners, check slippers flapping against his … her … its heels. Then suddenly both entities decided to stop. Nothing extraordinary confronted them. It was just a gas tank. A shiny new gas tank. All orange and brass. Not a single paint bubble or rust ring.

Meg sank to the wet ground, tugging Lowrie with her. Life and death were repeating themselves like some sort of cosmic joke.

'I don't want to be old,' she croaked, tears dropping off the tip of her crooked nose. 'I don't want to be dead.'

Lowrie didn't speak. There wasn't much you could add to that. It pretty much covered the way he was feeling too.

Me neither, he thought.

And somehow Meg heard him. Like a voice in the back of her mind. A gremlin in her head. And that wasn't all, a lifetime of vague feelings were invading her own. There were weddings and funerals, and pain in her leg, and terrible loneliness. She didn't want it. Any of it. She was only fourteen, for God's sake. She'd be only fourteen forever.

I want to leave this body, she thought. Just float out, the

same way I came in. And that's what she did, detached herself like a wet Band Aid, flopping to the tarmac beside a suddenly exhausted Lowrie McCall. The old man's lungs were pumped to bursting, and his legs shook like reeds.

'For a second there ...' he puffed. 'For a second there, I was ...'

'What? You were what?' asked Meg, just for something to say. She didn't care about the old man's troubles, she had worries of her own.

Lowrie swatted a sheet of rain from his forehead. 'I was alive again.'

And, for some reason, this made the old man cry like a baby. Meg thought she knew why. There was something wrong with Lowrie McCall. Something besides arthritis and bandy legs. A feeling had soaked through her ... whatever it was that she had now instead of skin ... while she'd been inside the old man. A feeling that reminded her of the tunnel.

That probably wasn't a good sign.

'Come on,' she said. 'Let's go inside. You'll catch your death.'

The tears blended with the rain dribbling over Lowrie's chin.

'Good one,' he nodded, a wry smile flickering around the corners of his mouth. 'Catch my death. You're a howl, you are. Here, give me a hand up.'

Meg stretched out her fingers, but caught herself in time.

'Oh no, old timer,' she said. 'No more bodysnatching for me tonight.'

Lowrie took himself off to bed, convinced he was experiencing some sort of prolonged hallucination. Meg, meanwhile, tried to familiarize herself with her new abilities.

There was bodysnatching and firing heavy objects around, for a start. So, whether or not she made contact with something was apparently up to her. A mental sort of a thing. Very Kung Fu altogether. If you wish it, it shall be.

After a few experiments, she discovered that everything had a bit of life in it. Even the old armchair had a few memories floating around inside its timber and foam. Most of them involved various bottoms and the functions thereof. Meg hurriedly decided against occupying any more furniture.

The stint inside Lowrie had cost her, though. Her aura was fainter now, she could feel a pull on her body. Not in any particular direction. Just somewhere else. Time was ticking on.

Spirits didn't sleep either, Meg discovered. What a waste of time. Here she was, her ghostly clock winding down, and your man was upstairs snoring his gob off. Typical grown-up. Nobody's time was worth anything besides his own.

She tried watching TV. But it was no good. Her supernatural eyesight picked out every electron on the screen. Focusing on the pictures took real concentration.

Food, then, was the only option left to her. Not that she was hungry or anything, it was just for something to do. She pilfered a chocolate mousse from Lowrie's fridge and scooped it out with her fingers. Disgusting certainly, but absolutely delicious.

And that was fine, just as long as Meg was actually concentrating on the mousse. But the second she stopped thinking about it, the sloppy goo began to float out through the walls of her stomach. Once they'd cleared her aura, gravity took hold and the dairy dessert splatted on to the chessboard lino.

Meg grimaced. Looked like she'd never be hungry again. But she'd never be stuffed either. Sighing mightily, the in-betweener lay on a threadbare sofa, being very careful not to think HOLE. Even so, memories of lost Smarties cried out to her from behind the cushions. There was a diamond ring down there too. Or there had been. It had belonged to Nora. Someone called Nora.

Lowrie inched down the stairs, eyes squinted for focus.

'Hello?' he called hesitantly. A stranger in his own house.

Meg sat up on the sofa. 'Who's Nora?'

Lowrie froze, one foot halfway between steps. 'Nora? Who told you about Nora?'

'The sofa,' said Meg simply.

Lowrie scanned her face for sarcasm, but found none. Why should there be? Apparently anything was possible. He limped heavily to the foot of the stairs, lowering himself, grimacing, into his easy chair. Meg could almost hear his bones creaking.

'Nora was my wife. We shared twenty-seven years of our lives.'

Meg sighed. Happy family stories always made her go mushy. 'You're lucky. To stay married that long.'

'Lucky?' snorted the old man. 'Easy to see you weren't married to her. She drank like a barrel of fish and smoked sixty cigarettes a day. Why do you think I live in this dump? That old sponge drank everything we had, including the furniture.'

'I suppose it was the drink that killed her in the end,' Meg said, trying to sound mature and sympathetic.

Lowrie nodded. 'In a way. She came home plastered one night, and drank a bottle of toilet bleach by accident.'

Now it was Meg's turn to look for sarcasm. Not a trace.

'And I'm just about getting me life in order, when in come you two and that big wolf of yours.'

Meg thought back to the tunnel. 'Oh, we're paying for our crimes. Believe me.'

'That other chap. Is he in … you know. Down below?'

'Yep,' nodded Meg.

'And what's your punishment?'

'I'm here listening to you, aren't I?'

'Oh, ha ha. You're a riot. Well, I'm glad you're taking death so casually.'

Meg sighed. 'I'm still alive. Only different. My life wasn't any great shakes, anyway.'

Lowrie nodded glumly. He knew the feeling.

'Can I ask you something?'

Lowrie nodded cautiously. 'I suppose so.'

'What's wrong with you?'

The old man paled. 'What sort of question is that?'

'Well, last night, when we were … joined … I felt something inside you. I dunno, something sort of bad.'

Lowrie snorted. '*Sort of bad?* Could you give me that in layman's terms?'

'Bad, dark … I don't know. I'm not a doctor.'

'Go on? Are you not?'

'Oh forget it!' scowled Meg. 'I'm sorry I asked.'

Lowrie rubbed the scar on his leg. 'It's my heart,' he said. 'The old pump is giving out.'

'Are you …'

The old man nodded ruefully. 'Yes. Couple of months. Six at the most.'

Meg squinted at him. 'Don't worry. Blue aura. Straight up to the Pearlies.'

'It's not the afterlife I'm worried about. It's this one.'

'It's a bit late for that.'

'You don't understand. Youngsters! Would you shut up and listen for once in your life … or death … or whatever.'

Meg swallowed a retort. Even uncharitable thoughts caused a dozen red shoots to sprout in her aura.

'OK. I'm listening.'

Lowrie pulled a spiral pad from his dressing-gown pocket.

'Me life's been a disaster. The whole thing. Not one high point to look back on. From marrying that old fish Nora, to getting me leg chewed by that beast.'

'There must have been something.'

Lowrie shook his head. 'Nope. I've made a hames of sixty-eight years. Every single decision I ever made was the wrong one.'

Meg allowed a big 'I doubt it' look to paste itself across her face.

'Take that face off you. It's hard enough explaining what a pathetic human being I am, without you sneering at my every word.'

'What do you want me to do? I can't go back in time or anything.'

'Oh,' said Lowrie, disappointed.

'I'll just help you around the house for a few days until my aura goes blue, and then poof, I'm off.'

'Will you shut up about yerself, and listen! I'm sure God Almighty didn't send you down here to do the dishes!'

Meg scowled. Old chaps thought they knew everything.

Here was this fellow spouting on about God, and he wasn't even dead yet.

'If you were sent back, it must be to do something special.'

A nervous feeling growled in Meg's spiritual stomach. 'Like?'

'Like help me sort out my life.'

You had to laugh. So Meg did. 'Sort out your life. What life? You've only half a year left.' It was the sort of thing Meg Finn did. Blurted out a mean statement like that, and then felt guilty for months.

'Well, I didn't mean ...' she stammered.

'No. You're right. What life? That's what I've been trying to tell you.' Lowrie's eyes were lost in past memories. 'If only ...'

He shook himself back to the present. 'Too late for if onlys. Time to do something about it.'

He opened the spiral pad. 'So, I've made a list.'

Ah! Point on the horizon, captain. 'What sort of list?'

'I divided my life into a series of mistakes. Things I didn't do when I had the chance. It wasn't easy, I'm telling you. There was a lot to choose from. But I've narrowed it down to four.'

The old man tore a page from the pad and handed it to the reluctant spirit. PAGE, thought Meg, and took the sheet. The surface was covered with barely legible scribbles. It didn't matter. The words sang out to Meg before she even attempted to read them. Even the squiggles were bursting with emotion. The pain of compiling this list swirled from the page in ropy, moaning memories.

There were at least twenty items on the list, most of which had been crossed out. That didn't matter to Meg. Their images leaked out through the ink-like ghostly reminders.

Lowrie wasn't exaggerating. His life had been a disaster. Marrying an alcoholic, living with her mother, not getting fire insurance for his first house. Arriving for a holiday in Yugoslavia on the day war broke out. It went on and on. These were things that couldn't be addressed. There was no helping them. But four items were ringed and numbered. Meg read them slowly, not believing what the spectral images told her.

At last, a puzzled soul looked up from the page. 'I don't get it,' she said simply.

'It's not too late for these,' said Lowrie, his face shining. 'They can still be done.'

Meg snorted. 'You're not serious.'

'Oh but I am, young lady. Regret is a powerful incentive.'

'I don't even know what you're talking about. I'm only fourteen, you know.'

Lowrie rubbed his scarred calf. 'With your help, I can accomplish these things. I never could before. But when you … possessed me yesterday, I felt young again. Ready for anything.'

'But these! I mean, what's the point? It's crazy.'

Lowrie nodded. 'To you, maybe. To everyone else on the planet. But these were *my* greatest failures. Now I have a chance to put them right, even if no one cares but me.'

Meg was running out of arguments. 'But what will it change, running around the country like a crazy man?'

'Nothing,' Lowrie admitted. 'Except my opinion of myself. And that, young Meg, becomes very important to a person as they grow older.'

Meg felt scowl wrinkles settle across her forehead. She hated that 'you'll understand it when you're older' chestnut. Especially now, as she wasn't getting any older. Ever.

She waved the flimsy sheet at him. 'It has to be this? We

have to travel the length and breadth of Ireland to complete four idiotic tasks? Nothing else will do you?'

'That's it,' replied Lowrie. 'That's the deal. That list is the only way to heaven,' he paused pointedly, 'for either of us.'

Belch was back. Sort of. Sort of Belch, and sort of back. Confused? He wasn't. Myishi had downloaded a complete 'virtual help tutorial' module into his memory. Now all he had to do was think of a question and a cyber demon would search the implants for hits. Like having a swot in your head. Just like it should be. Let the real men do the real work, and the nerds play with their toys.

The Devil himself had dropped in to the departure lounge to see Belch off. For the first time since the Mettallica concert, Belch was impressed.

Satan was wearing his Rough Beast form and wasted no time filling the new arrival in on the urgency of this mission. He grabbed Belch by the throat and pinned him to the cave wall.

'Go back. Find the girl. Make her bad. Quickly.'

The Devil's eyes were round and red. Screaming souls swirled in the irises. You had to admire effects like that.

Grandstander, thought Beelzebub, quietly.

'Make her bad?' enquired Belch respectfully.

Beelzebub winced. The Master didn't do questions.

Satan's grip tightened on Belch's windpipe and the canine in him whimpered involuntarily. Sparks sizzled around the Beast's sinewy frame, singeing Belch's matted fur.

'Bad!' Satan growled. 'Make her bad.'

'Fine,' gasped Belch. 'Make her bad. Got it.'

'Hurrggh,' grunted the Devil doubtfully, dropping Belch to the marble floor.

'If not ...' Satan left the sentence unfinished, vaporizing a passing spit turner to make his point.

Belch swallowed. That was clear enough.

'Yes, Master,' bobbed Belch. 'Consider her baddened.'

'Hurrggh,' grunted the Lord of Darkness again, and you'd be amazed the amount of expression he could pack into that single syllable. Then, in a flash of crisped flesh and ozone, the Beast was gone.

Beelzebub crossed to a lift door and pressed B for basement. Belch followed in his strange half-and-half lope.

'Technically, you don't have to *make her bad*, as the Master so eloquently put it,' explained Beelzebub. 'You just have to stop her being good. The target will have been sent back to help the old man. Your mission is to make sure her efforts fail. That way we get a red aura, blah di blah di blah. The Master gets his precious soul, I keep my job and you escape an eternity in the barbecue section. And − it ain't beef bein' cooked down there, cowboy.'

Beelzebub liked to think of himself as humorous. Black humour, naturally. He was, after all, a demon. He chuckled gently at his own joke. Belch was encouraged to join in the laughter by the sparks jittering around the teeth of Number Two's trident.

'There's one thing I don't get in all this,' ventured Belch.

'Only one?' sniggered Beelzebub, on a roll now.

'Yer man ...'

'The Master?'

'Yeah, him. Well, he's got me, hasn't he? What does he want that girl for?'

Beelzebub had an answer for that one, but he couldn't even think it this close to the inner chamber. Suffice to say it contained the words 'stubborn' and 'mule'.

'The Master believes Meg Finn to be special. Real potential. She did something to her stepfather apparently.'

Belch swallowed. 'Oh, that. Nasty stuff.'

The lift doors dinged open. Belch stepped in gingerly, half-expecting some collapsing trapdoor – ha ha you're not really going back at all – type of thing. But no, just solid floor. Carpeted with some pinkish hairy material. Better not to think about that.

'How long have I got? To make her bad.'

Beelzebub shrugged. 'It depends. Take it easy on the possessions, don't call home too often, and you've got enough juice for a week.'

Belch whined.

'Any problems, check the virtual help. Myishi assures me every eventuality is covered.'

'OK, boss,' said Belch compliantly, thinking that he'd be off like a bullet as soon this lift spat him out on planet Earth. Sayonara hell, and farewell stumpy demon in the girly dress.

'It's a kaftan,' said Beelzebub coolly.

'Woof,' croaked Belch. Seemingly, his quadruped side dominated in times of stress.

'That's right,' continued hell's Number Two. 'I can read minds. Only weak ones, granted, but you're smack bang in the middle of that category. Don't even think about escape, because the second your life force runs out you'll be snapped back here like a pooch on an elastic leash.'

'Right.'

Beelzebub primed his trident for a level-four whammy.

Very nasty. 'And you know I can't let you off with that girly dress crack, don't you?'

Belch shook a shaggy head. 'Arf arf.'

'My thoughts exactly,' grinned the demon, jabbing his buzzing staff into Belch's expectant skin.

So Belch was back. Spewed from the mouth of a sweating lift. Back where it all began; correction, back where it all ended. The granny flats' gas tank.

Very nice it was too. All orange and shiny, with barely a sign of the tragedy that had occurred there. Except for a hundred shrapnel gouges in the surrounding walls.

Belch had a big advantage over his adversary, because he knew exactly what was going on. His implant had filled him in on no end of spiritual trivia. For example, the only reason he could come back at all was because of the untimely riddling of his torso with metal fragments. This left him with decades of unused life essence, or soul residue. Unfortunately, life essence without a life is like a brain outside a skull: fragile and quick-drying. A day per decade was about all you got. Even with the booster shot, that left him a week max to complete his mission.

He also knew what Meg had to do to put a little blue in her aura. And it would be his absolute pleasure to put a stop to that. That little turncoat had cost him his life. So he would make absolutely sure that Meg Finn wouldn't be spending eternity sipping chocolate milkshakes on some cloud up at the Pearlies. No sir. She'd be turning a greasy spit in hell, and getting the odd lick of Belch's whip to keep her moving. Belch chuckled, a throaty growl. That was one image that appealed to him enormously.

So Belch had a plan. He would mosey over to the old

coot's flat, frighten him to death and then poor little Meggy wouldn't have anyone to help. Genius.

'Won't work,' said an electronic voice.

Belch glanced up. The virtual help floated at shoulder height, with a condescending sneer stretching its five-hundred-pixels-per-centimetre lips. The sneer looked like it belonged there.

'You're Myishi, I suppose? I've been told about you.'

The icon blinked and flickered. 'Yes ... and no.'

Belch groaned. Great. A schizophrenic computer program. (Obviously what had been Belch Brennan didn't think the word 'schizophrenic', but that was the general idea.)

'In terms of brain power, I *am* Myishi. His thoughts and expertise have been programmed into my memory. Spiritually, the Great One's soul still resides in Hades.'

Belch scratched the nub of flesh on his crown where the implant had been inserted. 'Best place for him, the maniac.'

The diminutive animated icon tutted. 'Do not disrespect the inventor. I will be forced to activate the ectonet and send a live feed. This, in turn, will most definitely lead to a pain surge in your mainframe.'

'Ectonet? Mainframe? What the hell are you?'

The impeccably dressed figure bowed. 'I am your Ecto-Link and Personal Help program. You may refer to me as Elph.'

Belch squinted at him. 'You're not draining my juice, are you?'

'No. I come free with the package.'

'Good. Now, what's wrong with my plan?'

The condescending sneer returned. 'It is the plan of an idiot. To kill the old man now does not make Meg Finn bad. If she has not tried, she cannot fail. For the target to fail, her essence must turn red.'

'Hmm,' growled Belch, absently scratching behind his ear.

'What you must do is foil their plans. Whatever McCall asks Finn to do, you must see to it that she fails.'

Belch nodded. Made sense. In a Spockish sort of a way.

'Right. Let's check out the flat then, see if we can't throw a spanner in the works.'

Elph frowned. 'I am not equipped with hardware implements.'

'Not a real spanner, cartoon head! A pretend one — you know, like "strong as a horse", except you're not really a horse.'

The megabyte sprite bobbed along beside him. 'Ah yes, Belch-san. I see. You speak metaphorically. This file was not included in my memory. The honoured Myishi did not feel it relevant to our mission.'

Belch snarled. 'The honoured Myishi can take his file and ...'

Before he could finish his highly graphic and uncomplimentary sentence, Belch's brain spasmed with a jolt of fiery pain. Not an actual brain, obviously — that was lying mouldering in a cheap pine box. But spiritual pain is every bit as excruciating as the physical kind.

After several moments Belch's ears stopped ringing. Elph was regarding him coolly.

'Disrespecting the Great One activates punitive feedback. It is not wise.'

'Woof,' grunted Belch. 'I mean, really.'

'There is no need to revert to English,' commented Elph. 'I am fluent in fourteen canine dialects, including the limited vocabulary of the pit-bull breed.'

Belch grunted. 'Let's get on with this, then. The old man's flat is just around the corner.'

'*Hai*, Belch-san.'

They proceeded through the courtyard, Belch upending rubbish bins, benches and even small cars, generally overdoing the poltergeist thing. Elph hovered at his shoulder, shaking his flickering head, and looking very disapproving for a hologram.

CHAPTER 5: MAKEOVER

NORA had apparently drunk the car, so they had to make the trip to Dublin by train. Being a pensioner like he was, Lowrie only had a pass for the second class, and so had to hold conversations with an invisible spirit while everybody watched.

'What's this trip about, McCall?'

Lowrie came back from whatever dream he was dreaming. 'Hmm?'

'Kissy Sissy. The first thing on the Wish List. What does that mean?'

The old man fired her a crabby glare. 'What it says. There's a woman called Sissy; I have to kiss her.'

'Yes. But why?'

'Never mind why. You just do what you were sent to do.'

Meg frowned, levitating ten centimetres off the seat. 'I'm trying to help, you know. A bit of manners wouldn't kill you.'

'Manners, is it?' snorted Lowrie. 'What sort of manners would that be, now? The sort where you break into someone's house and cripple them for life? Or the sort where you play a cruel and malicious trick on your stepfather?'

Meg felt herself fuming at the mere mention of Franco's title. 'Who told you about that?'

'The man himself.'

'You met Franco?'

Lowrie shifted on his seat. 'He came around to apologize after the ... accident.'

Meg could feel her molecules vibrating. Even in the afterlife, that man could drive her demented in one second flat.

Lowrie drove the nail home. 'The poor chap. And to think, I thought I was badly off.'

Meg couldn't believe her ears. 'He had you feeling sorry for him?'

'After what you did?'

'He deserved it!' hissed Meg. 'He deserved it, and more!'

'I dunno,' sniffed Lowrie, 'if anyone deserves that. That was ...'

'Justice,' announced Meg. 'It was justice. That creep sold my Mam's jewellery. Sold her charm bracelet that we used to add to every year. And he watched *our* telly, and sat on *our* sofa. He sat on our sofa so much that it wasn't ours any more. It was his. With his big, disgusting bum-print right in the middle.'

Lowrie read the girl's face. 'And did he give you the odd clatter?'

There was silence for a moment, and Meg settled back on to the cracked seat. 'Never mind changing the subject on me, McCall,' she said suddenly. 'Who's this Sissy woman? And how do you know she won't split your bony face in two when you try to plant one on her?'

Lowrie settled back against the window, pulling a sausage-like cigar from his breast pocket.

'Sissy Brogan,' he sighed, spinning the wheel on an ancient oil lighter. The flame, when it caught, was as least as pungent as the cigar. Meg watched, fascinated, as the smoke passed through her abdomen.

'Sissy Brogan was the woman I should have married. Never mind that old fish, Nora. Sissy was a real woman. They broke the mould when they made her ...'

'What mould? Like a jelly mould?'

'No.'

'Plaster?'

'Shut up, will ye?' growled Lowrie, his flow interrupted. 'It's an expression. It means she was unique. The one and only.'

'Oh.'

'We went stepping out once ...'

'Out where?'

Lowrie could feel a headache coming on. 'It's an expression! On a date! I took her on a date!'

'Right.'

'First of all to the pictures on O' Connell Street.'

'What was on?'

Lowrie scowled. 'I don't remember ...' he began, then the lines on his brow softened. 'It was *The Mask of Zorro*. I do remember.'

'Big deal. Sure that's still on.'

'I remember because I was doing all the sword-fighting bit on the way for chips. Sure, I was only a young lad.'

Meg chuckled. 'You? Acting the maggot. I don't believe it.'

'I barely believe it meself. Maybe the old brain is filling in the gaps for me. Anyway, it was a great night. A classic. They don't come along every day. You get maybe half a dozen in a lifetime. Perfect days. I can see her now, with the red hair curling behind her ears. The height of fashion in those days.'

'Yeah,' muttered a thoroughly bored Meg. 'That and outdoor toilets.'

But Lowrie was far too immersed to be distracted by smartalecry. His memories floated out of him. Wafting in luscious shades from his face and painting vague shapes in the air.

'A perfect day ...'

'But?'

'But I made a hames of it. As usual.'

'How? It sounds as though all you had to do was walk her home, give her a kiss goodnight and ...'

'I never kissed her.'

'You eejit.'

Lowrie shook his grizzled head ruefully. 'I know. Don't you think I know? Not a day goes by. It was my hands, you see.'

'Hands?'

'They were sweating. Real bad. Like two lilies on a pond. I was afraid to put them around her waist. Stupid, I know. Stupid.'

He got no argument from his ghostly partner.

'I thought the feel of two big, sopping palms would put an end to my chances. I thought — tomorrow, when it's cool and my hands are dry. So I left it and went home.'

'And you never saw her again?'

The old man smiled mirthlessly. 'Oh I saw her, all right. I saw her every day for four years. I saw the hurt in her eyes, then the coldness. I watched her marry my boyhood friend. And I had to stand there smiling, and hand over the ring like I was the happiest best man in the world.'

'If all this happened when you were young, then this Sissy must be ancient by now. When was the last time you were in touch with her?'

Lowrie scratched his bristled chin. 'Personally? Now you're asking. Must be the bones of forty years.'

Meg vibrated ten centimetres off the seat. 'Forty years! She could be dead, or living in a home or anything.'

'Oh no. Sissy is alive, all right. That much I do know.'

'And how can you be so sure? Seeing as your own brain was no great shakes the last time I was in there.'

Lowrie spoke clearly. 'Because Sissy's married name is Cicely Ward. And that's one even a hooligan like you should recognize.'

Meg sank dumbfounded into the foam of the train seat. '*That* Cicely Ward?'

'Yes, that Cicely Ward. She wasn't always who she is now, you know, she was herself once.'

Funnily enough, that made perfect sense to Meg. 'So, you're telling me that you had the chance to marry the country's favourite TV granny, and you blew it.'

Lowrie rapped his knuckles against his own thick skull. 'Yep. That's what I'm telling you.'

Meg whistled. 'You really have the knack, don't you? I thought my life was miserable.'

'Least I have a life.'

'Not for long.'

Lowrie pulled himself together. His memories whooshed back into his face like paint down a drain.

'Exactly. Not for long. So, if you'll just do what I say, I don't think there's any need for conversation.'

'But …'

'Never mind yer buts. You're only here 'cause you have to

be. If it was up to you, you'd be off burgling someone's castle in heaven.'

And with that Lowrie pulled his cap over his eyes and settled in for a snooze. Sleep again? Meg couldn't believe it. After all the snoring he did last night. How could someone with half a year to live bear to waste any of it sleeping? She shook her fist at the heavens. Thanks very much. Thanks a million. My last chance at salvation, and you send me to the one person that hates me more than Franco.

When the train pulled into Heuston Station, Lowrie was still dragging ragged breaths through his open mouth. Meg was getting fairly sick of looking at his fillings. It was like some medieval dentist had plugged the holes with lumps of coal. And just look at the state of him, she thought. Nora must've drunk his fashion sense along with everything else. If he went strolling around the streets of Dublin like that, people were going to start giving him their spare change.

There was zero chance of getting into the RTÉ television studio with Mr Sleeping Tramp there. Something had to be done. Cicely Ward's people weren't going to let a scruffy old mumbling eejit in to see their boss just because he blew a chance to kiss her back in the black-and-white movie days. And you may bet she had *people*; all these stars had groups of muscley types making sure they never had to talk to their fans.

Meg could just imagine Lowrie. Uh, em, please can I go in, because I've got a Wish List and there's this invisible spirit floating over my head … whack, bounce, skid along the pavement.

No. If they were ever going to tick anything off this list, it was up to her.

Time for a bit of possession. Meg steeled herself and

eased into Lowrie's slumbering frame. That's not so bad, she told herself. Now that you know what's going on.

The old man's brain was calm. Richly coloured images floated around like fantastic clouds. Dream on, old timer. No need to wake up. You wouldn't like what's going to happen anyway. Meg stretched her creaking legs and stepped down on to the platform.

Behind her, two nuns blessed themselves and prayed fervently that they would never end up like that poor old tramp babbling at thin air.

Belch was smiling wolfishly. It gave him a warm, fuzzy feeling to know that he could invade anyone's privacy at will. HOLE, he'd thought, and floated straight through Lowrie McCall's front door. Marvellous.

'They are not here,' buzzed Elph.

Belch ran a thin tongue over his incisors. 'I can't turn you off, I suppose?'

Elph blinked to access a file. 'I cannot be disconnected by the host. Any attempt would be met with a massive cranial discharge and immediate relocation to base.'

'I go straight to hell, is what you're trying to say.'

'Correct.'

'Just great. Well, could you please shut up while I search this place?'

Elph smiled, as a toddler would at an insect he is about to flatten. 'I will, as you say, shut up. But only because it is the most effective course of action.'

Belch rooted around in the threadbare furnishings for a while, then decided it was too much like hard work. He flopped on to the sofa, plonking ghostly Doc Marten's on the glass surface of an ancient coffee table.

'This place is a dump,' he remarked. 'Dunno why I bothered breaking in here in the first place.'

Elph blinked again, scrolling through Belch Brennan's case file. 'Doubtless because you are a dullard. My log informs me that you were prone to acts of extreme idiocy.'

Belch jumped off the sofa, sending it crashing into the wall. 'I knew a teacher like you. All smart comments and saying I was thick. Well, I fixed him, all right. Slashed his tyres, and scratched his bonnet.'

Elph nodded. 'Yes. I have video. I see you scratched your own name into Mr Kehoe's paintwork. Ingenious.'

'I'll fix you,' growled Belch, lunging for the hologram.

'I doubt it,' sneered Elph as the dog-boy passed through his electrical impulses. 'I am an intangible projection. In order to "fix me", you would have to remove your own head and bury it on holy ground. Unlikely, to say the least.'

Belch extracted himself from the wall, casting a vicious eye at his supposed helper. 'Righto, Mr Elph. Truce for now. But some day …'

'I suggest we look for clues as to our quarry's whereabouts.'

'Clues?'

'Ask the furniture.'

'Are you trying to be funny?'

Elph sighed. 'No, moron. Residual memories. Spirits are very receptive to them.'

'You do it, then. I don't fancy having a chat with a three-piece suite.'

'I am not a spirit. I am an …'

'I know, I know. An intangible projection, whatever that is. OK, but if you're having a laugh at my expense, then I might just have to remove this implant myself. How much deader can I get?'

Belch faced the battered sofa. 'Well, sofa,' he mumbled, feeling a complete fool, 'any idea what Finn and that old crusty are up to?'

He waited, half-expecting the raggedy old cushions to form themselves into a mouth and answer him. Instead, Meg appeared on the settee. Not Meg exactly. More like a painting of her, with the colours swirling of their own accord.

'Good,' said Elph. 'A grade-four residual memory. Quite recent.'

'Oh shut up, Spock. I'm trying to make out what she's doing.'

'Any aural input?'

'Huh?'

'Can you hear her?'

Belch listened, his pointed ears twitching in concentration. Words flowed from Meg's mouth like multicoloured birds. The colours were dark. Finn had not been happy: 'It has to be this? We have to travel the length and breadth of Ireland to complete four idiotic tasks? Nothing else will do you?'

'Pardon?'

'That's what she said.'

Elph hovered thoughtfully. 'So, the old man has set tasks. Doubtless they have already departed on their quest.'

'How much of a head start do they have?'

'Difficult to say. Time works differently on the spirit level. Judging by the memory dissipation, I'd say perhaps six hours.'

Belch tried a sarcastic chuckle. What came out was more of a poodle yip.

'Six hours? They could be out of the country by now. Well, that's it then. There's no way to find them. Might as well just sit here and watch a bit of telly until they come back. If ever.'

Elph chewed a holographic lip. It seemed as though the halfwit was correct. The old man had defeated them simply by leaving his house. How infuriating. Myishi would not be happy if his prototype failed him. The hologram could well be demoted to a microwave for Beelzebub's curries.

Belch flicked through the stations looking for some cartoons. News, news, ads. Rubbish. He was just about to switch off the set in disgust when a familiar face flashed on to the screen. It couldn't be … but it was.

A predatory growl rumbled in the back of his throat. How lucky can you get? Somebody down there liked him.

Meg strolled down O'Connell Street, enjoying the cool breeze on her scalp. Who'd have thought there was an advantage to being bald?

She knew exactly where she was. Mam used to bring her Christmas shopping here every year, before the accident. Got a day off school and everything. Clothes, toys, whatever she wanted, and topped off with a visit to McDonald's. The good old days.

Every now and then she caught a glimpse of herself in a shop window, and the shock reminded her of her mission. Get this old coot looking half-human so he'll have some chance of a smooch with Ireland's favourite grandmother.

A spot of shoplifting had been her first thought, but you can't shoplift a haircut. Plus, her aura had enough red in it already without her breaking a few more commandments. So Meg rifled her host's pockets. It was not a pleasant job. A bit like being a digger trawling through the dump. Her search yielded several crumpled tissues, lozenges from various decades, a comb covered in brylcreem and a pack of old bingo cards. Not exactly the oldest swinger in town. Finally Meg hit gold. Deep in the folds of a frayed wallet, she discovered a shiny new Visa card. Perfect.

The first zone of concern was the general head area. Lowrie had probably grown accustomed to it over the years but, seen through new eyes, it was a disgrace. Grey hairs sprouting from everywhere except the scalp. Eyes that had been rheumy and bloodshot since God knows when, and a raggedy stubble that broke the surface like wandering sandpaper. Something had to be done.

NU U was the answer. Her mother had taken her there once when she felt they were both in need of pampering. Manicures and facials all around, then home on the one-twenty feeling like a million dollars.

Meg pushed in the glass-and-steel doors. Her entrance to the NU U salon had the same effect as a gunslinger's into a western saloon. Frosty silence descended on the establishment. You could have heard a pin drop, and in fact did when a trainee hairdresser dropped several from between her teeth.

A black-clad blonde-headed young lady approached Meg warily. She kept her hands close to her chest in case they might accidentally brush against this unexpected visitor.

'Hi, I'm Natalie. May I help you?' was what her mouth said, but her eyes said: Get out before I call the police.

Meg cleared her throat. 'Do you do men here?'

Natalie nodded reluctantly. 'Yes … generally.'

'Good. Could you do this one then?'

Natalie blinked. 'Pardon?'

'Ah … me. Could you do me?'

'Our services are not inexpensive, perhaps the local barber …'

Meg flashed the credit card. 'Put the whole whack on this, Natalie.'

Natalie leaned in to examine the card. Not too close though. A relieved, almost charming, smile spread across her plum lips. 'Well, that seems to be in order. What would you like done?'

Meg snorted. 'I'd say now that's sort of obvious. I want the works.'

Natalie snapped her fingers, and two similarly clad assistants magically appeared at her elbows. 'This gentleman would like the works. And, if I might say so, not before time.'

Meg was whisked into a space-age chrome chair, and various beautifying machines were arranged around her head. Some she recognized: dryers, highlight lamps and electrolysis lasers. But others looked like they came straight off the bridge of the *Starship Enterprise*.

'Is this going to be noisy?' she asked nervously.

Assistant number one twittered delightedly. 'No, no. These are the very latest, all stealth-muffled for the patrons' comfort.'

Meg nodded. 'Good. Because I don't want to wake me up.'

By lunchtime Lowrie McCall had been plucked, shaved, moisturised, exfoliated, manicured, trimmed, coloured (burnished autumn, six-wash fade-out) and wrapped. All without rousing him from his slumber. Every time his consciousness twitched, Meg would simply tell it to go back to sleep. Gently, of course, without the usual rudeness she generally used with adults. The old man was only allowed to surface to sign the credit-card docket. And then only partially. Poor old Lowrie thought he was dreaming about winning the Lotto.

The transformation was phenomenal. Even Natalie was impressed. 'If it wasn't for the clothing, you could almost think Sir was a native Dubliner.' The highest compliment any Dubliner could pay to a culchie.

Right, next stop. New outfit. Time to introduce this old fossil to the twenty-first century.

The Stephen's Green Centre had always been Mam's favourite, so Meg dragged Lowrie's old legs along the length of Grafton Street and up to the second floor of the mall. She picked the shop with the loudest music pumping through the doors, and went in. Techno dance beats enveloped her immediately, inside her head – or McCall's head to be precise. Lowrie's mind stirred irritably in its sleep.

'Hush there now, off you go, no need to wake up just yet.'

A flat-headed nose-ringer slimed over to guide the old guy to the denture shop. 'You're in the wrong place, pops. This is a clothes shop. For people less than a hundred.'

Meg took this personally – after all, she was in the insulted body at the time. 'Pops?'

Nose-Ring swallowed, suddenly nervous. 'Well, you know, you being an oldish gent and all.'

Meg opened Lowrie's mouth to respond, and then found she couldn't. That creepy eejit was right. Maybe she belonged here, but Lowrie certainly didn't. You wouldn't put the Taoiseach or one of those other ancient fellows in combats and a bomber. Older people had their own fashions from the days before PlayStations. Sad-looking, but they were happy.

Meg speared Nose-Ring with a haughty glare. 'I was considering purchasing a gift for my … great-great-granddaughter, but now I shall take my big roll of cash somewhere else.'

Meg stormed out, delighted with the long words she'd used, and with the look on your man's face. Three doors down there was a place called Townsend's & Sons. Heaps of non-fashion in the window. Ties and everything. One of the plastic dummies even had a top hat on him. Oh, this was definitely the place for Mr Has-Been McCall.

She pushed in the door hesitantly, still thinking of herself as a young girl, who'd been hunted out of a dozen similar establishments in her short lifetime. A group of snobby-looking chaps were flitting around with measuring tapes hanging around their necks. None of them looked young enough to be the sons in Townsend's & Sons.

One strolled over. He had bits of chalk sticking out of his shirt pocket, and a droopy moustache like that chap in the Bugs Bunny cartoons.

'Sir?' he said, real cool, as if saying: Can I help you, sir? was too much effort.

Meg squinted. How should she put this? Be confident, she told herself. Like you belong here.

'Righto ... ah ... shop servant. I've had my head done by Natalie. Now I want a few decent things to wear. A suit or something. None of those top hats though, or he'll kill me. Well, he would if he wasn't too late.'

Meg giggled nervously.

'A suit, Sir? Any particular label?'

'No, just give me something expensive. Put the lot on my Visa.'

Suddenly there were smiles all round. Measuring tapes were whipped out like Indiana Jones bullwhips, and jammed up Lowrie's armpits.

'Would Sir prefer tailored or off the rack?'

'Em … not sure, just give me something already made up.'

'Very good. Stand still, please. Two- or three-piece?'

'Dunno. No waistcoat though.'

'Of course.'

'And a pair of those brown shoes. With the swingy yokes.'

'Tassels.'

'That's the ones.'

'Size?'

Tricky one. Time for some cute thinking. 'Size? I forget. The old memory is a bit banjaxed. Me being so ancient and all.'

'As long as Sir remembers how to sign his name.'

'Pardon?'

'Oh nothing. Just my little joke.'

Meg felt as though she were being dressed by a whirlwind. Father and sons flashed around her, shouting incomprehensible figures and phrases.

After several interminable minutes of poking and fitting, the tailors stopped their feverish activity.

'*Et voila!*' The elder Townsend admired his creation.

Meg risked a peek. Not bad, she supposed. Lowrie's threadbare outfit had been replaced by a navy jacket and grey trousers. The turn-ups fell perfectly on to a pair of dark brown, tasselled, lace-up shoes. The shirt was crisp and pale blue, and complemented by a deep red tie.

'Sir?'

The Townsends hovered round their client. Awaiting a compliment as vultures await a desert fatality.

'Em … It's eh …'

'Yes?'

Now then, what would James Bond say in this situation? 'Outstanding, gentlemen. Bang up job.'

This seemed to do the trick, and the Townsends fell to twittering amongst themselves. Papa approached with a small silver plate. Here came the bad news. And it was bad news. Very bad. Eight hundred and forty pounds! If poor old Lowrie had any idea what was going on, this would have killed him for sure.

She handed over the Visa card, hoping that dying in debt didn't colour your aura. If it did, Lowrie was in big trouble.

A son glided over. He held Lowrie's old clothes out in front of him in a carrier bag, like a nurse with a nappy sack.

'Does Sir wish to have these ... things?'

Meg considered it. She'd already removed the wallet, the train ticket, pension book, keys and measly few bob.

'Nope. Sir doesn't. Bin the lot of them.'

'A wise choice.'

No turning back now. It was these swanky new clothes, or try to get into RTÉ in his underwear. And there was a sight the free world wasn't ready for yet.

It was time to wake the old man up. Meg eased herself from his body and waited for the fireworks. The old green eyes blinked dreamily and a slow smile spread across Lowrie McCall's lips.

'Hello,' he mumbled, to no one in particular.

Strange behaviour. The Townsends all clustered at the far wall.

Lowrie raised a finger. 'There's something familiar about you.'

Meg looked around. Who the hell was the old guy talking to?

'I never forget a face.'

What face? Maybe the possession had pushed Lowrie over the edge. She followed his bleary gaze. The dozy eejit was talking to his own reflection in the full-length mirror. A whoop of delighted laughter burst from her mouth.

The familiar irritated crease appeared in McCall's brow. 'What are you laughing at?'

The Townsends flushed; they had indeed been tittering discreetly at their latest customer's behaviour.

Meg swallowed her giggles. 'Oh nothing, apart from the fact that you're talking to yourself in the mirror.'

'Don't be ridiculous! That's not me.'

'Take a closer look, McCall, it's you all right.'

Lowrie studied the suave figure in front of him. It did indeed seem that there was a frame surrounding the gentleman. Most unusual. Unless of course the figure was a reflection.

'Oh dear,' he sighed, the penny finally dropping. 'This is who I could've been.'

Meg snorted. 'God Almighty, McCall. You can turn anything into a whingeing session. You're supposed to be happy.'

Lowrie touched the glass, just to make sure. 'I am happy. This is ... unbelievable. Thank you.'

'Welcome. Anything to give you a better chance of snagging Cicely Ward.'

'For a second there I thought you did this for me.'

'I did. You really are a moody old coot. Do you never just smile, and not worry about the consequences?'

Lowrie smoothed his silk tie. 'I used to. A lifetime ago ... before ... before everything.' A sudden thought struck the old man. 'Here, how did you pay for all this?'

Somehow, even without a drop of blood in her veins, Meg managed to blush. 'I didn't.'

'Oh no. You used my body to hold up this shop!'

'I did not!'

'Then what?'

Meg floated ahead of him out the door. 'Never mind. We have to get out to RTÉ, remember? It's out in Donnybrook.'

Lowrie ran under his own steam for the first time in years. 'Come back here, you. Tell me the truth!'

'OK, then. But you're not going to like it.'

'I don't care. Tell me anyway.'

Meg told him. He didn't like it.

CHAPTER 6: **KİSSY SİSSY**

THEY took a bus to the RTÉ studios. Even Lowrie had a few layers knocked off his grumpy shell by sitting on the top deck. It was a bright spring day in the city, and the streets flowed by beneath their window like a river of life. Of course Lowrie, being Lowrie, couldn't stay happy long.

'Listen, spook. Where's my other stuff?'

'Binned it.'

'What? I've had that jacket nearly twenty years!'

'I know, it told me.'

This being Dublin, no one was too concerned about some old fellow chatting to himself on a bus.

'You had no right!'

'Are you serious about this Kissy Sissy thing or not?'

'Dead serious, if you'll pardon the expression.'

'Well, she's hardly going to smack the gob on some old eejit lugging around a carrier bag full of smelly rags. And I'll tell you another thing, you're lucky those Townsend chaps didn't sell underwear, or your century-old shorts would've been for the chop as well.'

Lowrie blanched. 'How did you …?'

'Yes, I saw your old stringy vest. And it's a sight that'll stay with me for the rest of my …' Meg trailed off, suddenly realizing just how dead being dead was.

'I know, Meg,' said Lowrie, calling her by name for the first time. 'We all think we're going to live forever. Then bang! Our time is up and we haven't done any of the things we thought we'd do. Well, not me. I've got a chance to redeem myself. And a partner to help me do it.'

Meg sniffled, even though there were no tears on her cheeks. 'Partner?'

'You.'

'I'm only here because I have to be, remember?'

Lowrie nodded. 'I know that, but maybe your heart is in it all the same.'

'No, McCall. Don't rely on me. There's no point. I could never help anyone, even myself.'

'Now, who's moaning?'

'Ah put a cork in it, soppy.'

'Charming. Didn't you ever learn to respect your elders?'

'You're too old to be an elder. You're an older elder.'

'Very funny. If I was a hundred years younger …'

And so the first tendrils of a bond crept between the body and the spirit. And, though Meg Finn didn't notice it, a few more strands of blue ignited in her aura.

The RTÉ studios had security on the gate. A big Dublin bruiser with cropped hair and zero tolerance for chancers.

'Go away. Far away,' said the guard, whose tag read Dessie.

'Hold on there now a sec,' protested Lowrie. 'I'm here to see Cicely Ward.'

The guard looked up from his clipboard. 'Yeah, you and every other lovestruck old fool.'

Lowrie decided to have a go at indignant.

'Pardon me, young man, but Missus Ward happens to be a close personal friend of mine.'

'Sure, and I'm Leonardo di whatshisface.'

Even Lowrie recognized blatant sarcasm when he heard it. 'Did you never learn to respect your elders?'

'If I had a pound for every time I heard that line ...'

Don't talk to me, thought Meg.

'You old fellas are the worst, trying to scam your way in for a bit of celebrity-spotting. Go on, get out of it before I call the pensioners' police.'

Lowrie straightened his tie. 'Do I look like the kind of person who would need to scam his way anywhere?'

The guard rubbed the stubble on his scalp. 'Never judge a book by its cover. I myself have a first from Trinity in medieval poetry.'

Meg decided it was time to intervene. 'Use the power of your mind, Lowrie.'

'Pardon?'

Bandy hearing, thought Dessie. 'I said: never judge a book by its cover.'

'Not you!'

'Not me? Who then?'

'Tell him, Lowrie.'

'Tell him what?'

'Tell who what?'

It was all getting very confusing. Meg hovered beside the old man's ear.

'Just listen, McCall. Don't talk. While I was inside your head, I unlocked certain powers.'

'You did in your Barney.'

'What about Barney?' asked Dessie. 'We don't make Barney here. It's syndicated!'

'Use the power of your mind, Lowrie. Make this numbskull open the gate.'

Lowrie shrugged. This whole mind-control idea was no more incredible than anything else that had happened over the past twenty-four hours. He squinted fiercely at the guard.

'You will open the gate.'

'I doubt it.'

'Concentrate, McCall. Reach out with your thoughts.'

Lowrie gritted his teeth, focusing his will in a tight beam.

'You will open the gates, because I wish it!'

Dessie's eyes glazed over like two scratched marbles.

'Yes, Master.'

'It works,' crowed Lowrie. 'I'm a superbrain!'

'What's that, Master?' asked the guard. 'Turn you around and give you a swift kick in the behind? If that is your command.'

'I didn't think that!'

'No! I did. Now get out of here quick before I'm forced to call an ambulance, and take that voodoo rubbish with you.'

Lowrie glanced over his shoulder. Meg's ethereal frame was shaking with mirth.

'Oh ha ha, very funny.'

'Sorry,' spluttered Meg. 'Couldn't help it.'

'I should have known better.'

'Course you should,' agreed Dessie. 'I've heard every excuse in the book.'

Lowrie closed his eyes. Not a word to anyone in over a year, and now two conversations at the same time. 'Now, I'm never going to get in here.'

'You can sing that, grandad.'

Meg floated over beside the obstinate Dub. 'The way I see it, the brain is like a piano. You just have to push the right keys.'

She rolled up her sleeve and plunged her hand into the guard's ear. It disappeared up to the elbow.

'Urghh,' groaned Lowrie. 'That's disgusting.'

'Watch it now, you, I could turn nasty at any moment.'

Meg ground her teeth as she rooted around. 'Here it is now. Prepare yourself for complete obedience.'

Lowrie could almost hear the click as his partner pressed some internal switch. 'There we go.'

Dessie did indeed seem different. His knees began knocking together, and his hand jittered as though on puppet strings.

'Hmm,' mused Lowrie. 'You know who he reminds me of?'

'Yes, that rock 'n' roll singer with the hair.'

And without warning Dessie launched into an animated version of 'Blue Suede Shoes', complete with pelvic gyrations and wobbly lip.

'Oops,' said Meg. 'Wrong button.'

She tried again, like a bear feeling around for the hive. 'There, I think.'

No good. Now Dessie was whinnying like a horse.

'Oh, just possess him, for goodness' sake.'

'No chance. It's bad enough having your memories floating around my head. Never mind a whole heap of medieval poetry. Anyway, I've got it now.'

Click. And Dessie was docile as a kitten, big hairy arms swinging at his sides.

Lowrie coughed painfully. 'Desmond. Would you kindly open the gate?'

Dessie grinned. 'Sure, man. And do you know why?'

'No, Desmond, why?'

A tear crept from the corner of the guard's eye. 'Because I love you, man. I love you and all the little flowers, and I love the double-decker buses, and I even love the students from Trinity with their smelly coats and smart comments. I love the universe, man.' Sobbing gently, Dessie buzzed open the gate, rubbing the mechanism fondly.

'Oh, Desmond. Could I have a visitor's pass, please?'

'Sure, man. And why don't you crash in my pad later, man? We could absorb some vibes.'

'That sounds very interesting,' said Lowrie, with absolutely no clue as to what the guard had just said. He turned to his floating partner. 'What did you do to that poor chap?'

Meg shrugged. 'I just saw a pink happy-looking box at the back of his head and opened it up.'

'I think I preferred him as a bruiser.'

Lowrie strolled down the broad driveway, his confidence growing with each step. With the pass clipped to his lapel, he could freely infiltrate every area of the studios, including, he hoped, the 'Tea with Cicely' set.

TV sound stages look different in real life. Smaller for a start. And on telly you don't see the edges. It was as though some giant had taken a bite out of a suburban house and then, realizing the decor was horrendous, spat it out in Donnybrook. Lowrie was a bit disappointed. It flowed out of him in violet streams.

Meg couldn't resist a dig. 'Ahhh. Did the baby think it was weal?'

Lowrie bit his tongue. He wasn't going to be ejected for insanity now. Not when he was so close.

Meg giggled. 'Bugs Bunny is not weal either. Just pwetty pictures that move weally fast.'

Lowrie shot her a warning gaze. And in Meg's world you really could shoot a gaze. Concentrated orange venom spiralled from the old man's eyes and splurged all over her head.

'Hey! Give it up!'

'Less of the wisecracks then,' hissed Lowrie, maintaining a pleasantly smiling face.

The audience consisted of the white-haired, blue-haired and no-haired. Their auras betrayed their true thoughts, though. Stories of struggle and pain mingled in the air above them in a gaseous tableau. Love was the predominant emotion. Love and family. Almost every soul held the face of a lost loved one precious in their mind.

The warm-up man stopped cracking lame jokes, listening to a message through his earpiece. He began clapping and screaming like a lunatic. The audience followed suit. Just the clapping. No screaming. This wasn't a Boyzone concert, after all.

'Here we go,' whispered Meg.

Lowrie mopped his hands with his new silk hanky. They were sweating like sponges.

Belch's canine smile stretched across his snout, revealing an unfeasible amount of teeth.

'I don't believe it,' he chuckled.

Elph flitted to his shoulder.

'Disbelief is often the reaction of the mentally challenged. That and superstition. All phenomena can be reduced to mathematical terms. Even heaven and hell can be expressed as spatial equations.'

Belch frowned. 'You are such a nerd, Pixie.'

'That's Elph.'

'Whatever.'

Elph blinked, accessing his thesaurus. 'Hmm. Nerd: geek, square, one unskilled in social interaction.'

'Just shut up and look at the television.'

Elph buzzed over to the screen. 'Ancient technology. Not even digital. Subject to environmental interference.'

Belch could feel an attack of doggy rage coming on. 'Never mind that! Just look at what's on the screen.'

Elph's eyes spiralled into zoom. 'A series of coloured dots, transmitted in specific order to create the illusion of …'

'Shut up!' howled Belch, leaping to his feet. 'Shut up! Shut up! Shut up! Arf arf aaaaarffff!'

Elph gave him a little shock, partly out of necessity, partly because he enjoyed it. 'Are we rational now?'

'Woof.'

'I'll take that as an affirmative. Now, what were you trying to tell me, in your own Cro-Magnon fashion?'

Belch patted a smoking patch of hair over his ear. 'Look. It's him. On the telly.'

The virtual help's eye lenses whirred again.

'You are correct. I have an eighty-nine per cent match-up probability.'

'He looks different. Not as pathetic as usual.'

Elph sank an immaculately manicured hand into the screen. Waves of red sparks rippled across the screen, obscuring the picture completely.

'What are you doing? This could be a … what do you call it? A Sherlock Holmes thing … a clue!'

Elph blinked, a pulse of light shimmered along his arm and into the television.

'I have located the signal,' he said presently. 'It is a live broadcast. I am relaying the coordinates back to the Master's mainframe.'

Belch could feel the saliva glands in his hooked jaws going into overdrive. The bloodlust was on him. This dog thing wasn't too bad.

'How soon can we be there?' he said, more than a hint of the hairy half in his tones.

'Look around you, cretin,' muttered Elph. 'You're already there.'

Cicely Ward swanned on to the sound stage, and poor old Lowrie nearly fell out of his seat. Four hundred knees creaked painfully as the audience rose for a standing ovation.

'Right so, Lowrie. What's the plan?'

McCall blinked a bead of sweat from his eye. 'Plan? You know. Kiss her.'

'That's it? Kiss her?'

'Well …'

'God. You're about as good a planner as your man Custer.'

Dark patches began to appear on Lowrie's shirt. 'I'm new to this sort of thing. I thought you'd help out.'

'*I'm* not kissing her. It was bad enough kissing my own granny.'

'You're dead right you're not kissing her. If there's any kissing to be done, I'll do it!'

'Correct.'

'Right.'

'Good.'

'OK so. When I give the word, you take over. Get me old bones down there and I'll do the rest.'

Meg nodded. 'I can do that. Now, shut up talking to yourself, they're sitting down.'

Cicely quietened the audience with a wave of her elegant fingers. She was a striking woman, tall with steel-grey hair and round brown eyes. It was easy to understand Lowrie's attraction.

'Good evening, my friends.' She winked conspiratorially. 'I have to pretend it's evening because of the Saturday repeat.'

It was vintage Ward. The editors would leave it in for both shows. The audience tittered fondly, their worries instantly forgotten.

'Our show this *evening* concentrates on an issue that has affected us all at one time or another. Today we're going to talk with our panel about lost love.'

Lowrie nearly threw up. His perspiration glands began to pump out the gallons.

'Lost love?' giggled Meg. 'This is unbelievable.'

'Oh no,' moaned Lowrie. 'It's too much. I can't.'

A concerned woman tugged at his sleeve. 'Are you all right, honey?'

Lowrie felt as though there was a footpump feeding into his brain. 'I'm OK. Thanks. Fine. I just need a bit of air.'

He stood on shaky legs, suddenly feeling ridiculous. New clothes? Kissy Sissy? What had he been thinking?

'Where are you going?'

'Home. Home. Where I belong!'

Meg hovered before his face. 'No! You can't. We've come this far!'

'Get out of my way!'

Of course they were in the middle of a row. Heads began to swivel on both sides.

'Sit down!'

'I can't.'

'What are you going to do? Run off home and die?'

The blood hammered in Lowrie's ears, drowning out his thoughts.

'Yes!' he shouted over the pounding. 'Yes! I'm going home to die!'

A statement like that gets everyone's attention pretty sharpish. There was total silence on the sound stage. Even the cameramen stopped chewing gum.

Cicely Ward shielded her eyes against the TV lights. 'Are you all right, sir?'

Lowrie's throat was dry, and his palms were wet. Typical.

'Let's do it!' said Meg.

'No …'

'No, you're not all right, sir?'

Big security guys were nonchalantly converging on B Section.

'Come on, partner! This is another wrong decision.'

'I can't.'

Cicely Ward squinted. 'Don't I know you?'

Lowrie took a deep breath and met her enquiring stare. 'Hello, Sissy.'

'Sissy? No one's called me that since … Oh my God – Lowrie?' The hostess made a faltering move backwards, almost tripping on a low step.

Security was hurrying now, making real professional-looking hand signals.

'Let's go, Lowrie!'

McCall stared at his girlfriend from nearly half a century ago. Her eyes were the same. The very same.

'OK, partner. Get me down there.'

'About time,' said Meg, sliding into the old man's frame. Lowrie instantly took a back seat, like a passenger on a fairground ride. But he could feel. He could feel the strength and passion of youth buzzing through his old frame.

'Hey, Sissy,' called Meg. 'You stay right there, honey. Lowrie's got ... I mean, I've got something for you.'

Inside his own head, Lowrie groaned. That girl watched too much American television.

The security dropped all pretence of composure, and charged like a herd of particularly annoyed rhino. Their leader seemed to be roaring up his sleeve.

'We gotta possible obsessive, Section B. Double quick.'

'Oops. Time to go.'

Meg hopped up on a back-rest, narrowly escaping the questing fingers of the nearest guard. Two more clashed heads, diving for where Lowrie's feet had been. She giggled. It was just like the time she'd had an entire rugby team chasing her for calling their jerseys girly. They hadn't caught her then either.

Careful not to snag the audience on their heads, Meg skipped down along the seat rests, very dashing in her tailored suit.

Cicely was staring in disbelief. 'Lowrie ... I ... Oh dear!'

Meg vaulted into the aisle. 'With you in a sec, dollface.'

Lowrie cringed. Dollface?

The cameramen recovered their composure, swivelling lenses like tank-turrets. This extraordinary old man could provide the shot of the year! One over-enthusiastic bouncer threw a punch. He pulled it though, not wishing to crush the old guy's skull. The delay gave Meg ample time to snatch a knitting basket and place it in the path of his fist. Judging by the yelps, the bouncer had made contact with a concealed pin cushion.

'*Olé*,' shouted Meg, drumming her heels dramatically.

'*Olé!*' shouted the crowd. They couldn't help it. Meg's enthusiasm was contagious.

A railing led to the stage floor. Tubular and smooth.

'Oh God no,' groaned Lowrie.

'I'm afraid so,' chuckled Meg and mounted the banister side saddle. She whooshed down its length, snatching a rose from a bedecked straw hat on her way past.

There was only one beefy obstacle left, and the boom man took him out trying to get the mike in over Lowrie's head.

'*Olé!*' shouted Meg

'*Olé*,' responded the audience.

Cicely's face was flushed. It was like something out of those old pirate films. That was what oldies liked, so that was what Meg was giving them.

She handed Cicely the rose. 'For you, my precious jewel.'

'Lowrie? Is it you? What are you doing?'

'What I should have done forty years ago.'

Meg swept the presenter into her arms. The audience was enthralled; hankies were popping out like weeds after rain.

It was perfect. Romantic, forbidden, exciting. Perfect. Then, of course, all hell broke loose.

Belch looked down. He was floating sixty metres above the ground.

'Arf,' he yelped. 'Arf arf ooowwwww!'

'Woof, eh eh ruff,' grunted Elph in flawless pit bull. Which translated as: Relax, cretin, you're already dead.

Belch licked a rope of slobber from his chin. 'OK, smart alec. It just takes a while to get used to all this death stuff. Zooming off all over the world.'

The hologram tried to explain. 'We are not solid matter, you see. Of course, strictly speaking, that's not exactly true, if you consider it at a sub-atomic level ...'

Elph paused, noticing the 'I have no clue what you're on about' look plastered across Belch's face. 'Or, to put it in dullard's terms, we can go wherever we want to, so long as we know exactly where that is.'

'Oh,' said Belch, not really any the wiser. 'Where I want to be is beside that old geezer with my fingers around his throat.'

Elph's telescopic eyes buzzed and zoomed, reading the impulses inside the wires.

'I believe I can isolate the precise signal.'

'Well, get on with it then, you blabbermouth fairy!'

'That's Elph!'

'Whatever.'

Elph's fingers extended and spliced themselves with the rubber-coated wire. Strands of energy whiplashed around the point of contact.

'Hang on.'

Belch barely had time to yip before they were hurtling through the meshed wires of the signal conduit. The hardware flowed around and through them. Belch could see electrons of electricity arguing with each other. He watched as the positive and negative ions were drawn irresistibly together. Not that they seemed to mind.

Then they emerged through the lens of a camera, and

into a full-scale riot. Hundreds of elderly people were on their feet, stamping and hooting. Dazed security men lay scattered around the studio rubbing injured parts.

Belch growled in the back of his throat. 'I like this place.'

'I'm glad to hear it,' commented Elph dryly. 'When you've finished admiring the decor, you might notice that our target is less than three metres away.'

Belch whipped his snout around, instantly recognizing Meg Finn's scent. She was here, inside the old man. Belch could feel the canine half taking over. Bloodlust rose in the back of his throat. Curved claws sprouted from his fingertips.

'I'll tear her aura right off!'

Flexing powerful hind legs, Belch launched himself through the air. He impacted like a pile-driver, knocking Meg straight out of Lowrie's body. The two spirits rolled across the stage, auras spitting sparks.

'Now, you dirty turncoat,' growled hell's angel, 'you're coming with me.'

'Where's that?' quipped Meg. 'The doghouse?'

The smart remark was instinct. What was left of Meg Finn was actually quaking in her ectoplasmic boots. Belch was different. Not just the dog bit, it was more than that. He looked meaner, smarter. Like he'd seen hell, and liked it.

'Ruff woof huh huh,' snarled the dog-boy. Which Elph could have translated as: that's the last joke you'll ever make, because I'm going to rip your tongue out!

Amazingly enough, even with absolutely no knowledge of canine dialects, Meg was able to get the gist. Perhaps it was the taloned fist hovering over her face that gave her a clue.

Elph's circuits were smoking with frustration. 'No you cretinous creature! Leave the girl. She has already played her part! Get the old man!'

It was no use. Belch was too immersed in his vengeance. The situation was shooting off at unforeseen tangents.

Lowrie was oblivious to all the spiritual mayhem. As far as he was concerned, everything was going according to plan. Meg had got him down here, perhaps in a slightly more ostentatious fashion than he would have preferred, but here he was. And now it was up to him to finish off item one on the Wish List, ie, Kissy Sissy.

Cicely Ward was stunned, as you would be if your boyfriend of nearly half a century hence turned up and made mincemeat of your security. In spite of that, she made no attempt to disentangle herself from Lowrie's arms. Arms which were beginning to ache from the strain.

'Well, Lowrie?' she said, echoes of the teenager in her voice. 'Why have you come here?'

It occurred to Lowrie then that he was probably on television.

'Lost love,' he said simply, and kissed her on the lips.

And the crowd went ape, especially when Cicely Ward draped a hand over the dapper old gent's shoulder and kissed him back. It was fantastic, stupendous.

An ethereal ray of white light exploded from the point of lip contact. It bathed the pores of every man, woman and spirit in the studio. Of course nobody realized that. They just knew that for a single moment everything was better in the world.

Elph knew it though. He could see the ray and he knew exactly what it was. Trouble. Major trouble.

Belch felt it too. The spiky hairs on his neck tingled a

warning. 'What the hell is that?' he growled, peering over his shoulder.

Elph just had time to answer before the ray of energy blasted them both back to the underworld.

'Good,' he said. 'Pure one hundred per cent good.'

Meg felt a rush of blue in her aura.

Cicely walked Lowrie to the gate, ostensibly to protect him from the twitching fingers of security.

'I can't believe it's you,' she said, tucking a curl behind her ear. 'Lowrie McCall standing right here in front of me.'

Lowrie sighed. 'I'm a few decades late.'

The television presenter took his hands in hers. 'Maybe. But not too late.'

Meg was busy trying not to throw up. 'Oh, puleeeze. Give up all the soppy rubbish, McCall. Give her another smacker and let's get a move on. We still have a long way to go.'

'Shut up. I'm busy.'

Cicely blinked. 'Sorry? What did you say?'

'Nothing. I was … eh … talking to my inner demons. It comes from spending too much time alone.'

'Stay, then. For a while at least. We have so much to talk about.'

For a second, Lowrie wavered. It was tempting. 'Eh … No. I have a few things to do. Important things.'

Cicely wiped a tiny tear from the corner of her eye. 'I understand. Will you be back?'

Lowrie hesitated. Just say yes, it would make everything much easier. 'No, Sissy. I don't think so.'

'I see. Well, it was lovely to see you again. Even if only for a minute. And if you do change your mind …' She pressed a card into his palm.

Lowrie hugged her close, her familiar perfume filling his head. 'Goodbye, Sissy.'

Her tears were wet against his cheek. 'Goodbye, old friend, and thanks for the ratings.'

Lowrie strolled out through the gate. Dessie was making a daisy chain on the lawn.

Lowrie paused, there was one more thing. 'Sissy,' he called.

She turned squinting, the sun in her eyes. 'Yes?'

'That night ...' stammered Lowrie, 'after the cinema, when I didn't kiss you. Do you ever wonder ...?'

Cicely smiled through her tears. 'Every day and night, Lowrie McCall, every day and night.'

CHAPTER 7: FOOTBALL CRAZY

THEY took the late bus north. Luckily, the upstairs was deserted.

'You didn't see a thing?' said Meg incredulously.

Lowrie scratched his chin. 'Nope.'

'But there was Belch, only he was half dog. And this little floating fellow with zoomy eyes, and then a huge explosion of white light that blew the two of them away but didn't hurt me a bit.'

'No. Didn't notice any of that.'

Meg scowled. 'Too busy with your *girlfriend*.'

Lowrie leaned back on the seat smiling. 'Say whatever you like, spooky. Nothing can put me in a bad mood today.'

'It's disgusting. All you old people running around kissing each other. Have you no dignity?'

'You wouldn't be jealous, by any chance?'

'Jealous? Of what? Kissing a granny?'

Lowrie sat up. 'No. Jealous of … I dunno … life? Being happy?'

Meg stared out the bus window, watching the city streets flash past. 'What sort of question is that to ask a fourteen-year-old? I don't think about that sort of thing. Just music and sweets.'

'Hrmmph,' grunted Lowrie doubtfully.

'Hrmmph yourself. I think I preferred you when you were a moody old git.'

Lowrie refused to be drawn. 'Would you tell me something, Meg?'

'I might.'

'What did he do to you?'

'Who?'

'You know who. Franco. What did he do, to make you do what you did?'

'Is that a tongue twister?'

'Seriously.'

'Seriously, it's none of your business.'

Lowrie nodded. 'Fair enough. I thought we were becoming friends.'

Meg wagged a finger. 'I know what you're doing. It's that guilt thing. My mam was always trying that on me. Well, it won't work. I don't want to talk about it.'

Lowrie relented. 'OK, partner. Some other time.'

I doubt it, said Meg's face. Rather than argue, she changed the subject.

'What's number two?'

Lowrie blinked. 'Excuse me?'

'Number two on the Wish List.'

'Oh. Right. I suppose you might have heard of Croke Park?'

'That old place? Where they play hurling and Gaelic football?'

'The very place. The greatest, most famous stadium in the country. A place full of history —'

'OK, I get the message. What about it?'

'I want to kick a football over the bar in Croke Park.'

Meg wasn't the least bit surprised. 'Of course. Why not? Are you sure you wouldn't fancy a spot of pole-vaulting too?'

'Positive, thanks, even though I know you're just being sarcastic.'

'I suppose there's a story behind this?'

'Yep.'

'I suppose it's long and boring too, just like the last one?'

Lowrie grimaced. 'Afraid so.'

'Let's hear it, then,' sighed Meg, settling into the bus's seat — not too far in, though.

Lowrie smiled. 'If you insist.' He pulled the inevitable cigar from somewhere and wedged it between his back teeth. No lighting it, though. Public transport.

'Back before the war —'

'Which war?'

'The World War.'

'First?'

'Second, smart alec. That's not important.'

'Couple of French people might disagree with you there.'

'To the story. It's not important to the story.'

'Getting a bit ratty, aren't we, Lowrie?'

'I wonder why? Anyway, back before the Second World War, my Dad decided to send me off to boarding school.'

'Has this got anything to do with the war?'

'No. Not really.'

'I knew that! And here I was, getting all excited about a war story.'

'It was for reference. Oh, forget it.'

'Sorry, Lowrie. Go on.'

'No.'

'Ah, stop sulking, and tell me the story.'

'Are we going to have to go through this every single time?'

Meg nodded. 'Afraid so. You're too old for me to be seen getting along with you.'

'I thought as much. Very well, I shall persevere. But only because I know that really you're dying to hear my story. It's just your pigheaded teenage mentality that keeps forcing you to interrupt.'

Lowrie began his tale. As he spoke, images flowed from his pores, swirling around his head like an impressionist's dream.

'I was a small kind of a lad with no brothers or sisters, so Dad decided that boarding school would toughen me up. Apparently that was the thinking in those days, back before Dr Spock —'

'What does the *Starship Enterprise* —'

'*Dr* Spock. Haven't you ever read a book?'

'I have!' retorted Meg, a little too forcefully. She didn't think it worth mentioning that she had never actually finished a book without pictures.

'So, at the age of eleven, I was carted off to Westgate College for Boys. A charming establishment packed with sadistic bullies and leather-swinging Christian Brothers.'

Meg nodded sympathetically. It sounded a bit like her estate.

'It was porridge for breakfast, and a sound thrashing for dinner and tea. There were only four subjects: Latin, Irish, sums and football. None of which were fortes of mine. Being neither rich nor a Dubliner, I quickly became one of the least popular boys in school.'

'This is not by Charles Dickens, is it?' interjected Meg, trying to sound literary. In fact she'd seen *Oliver* about twenty times. It had been her mam's favourite.

'But I had my chance to fit in. After six months of hell, an opportunity came my way ...'

'Let me guess. You blew it?'

Lowrie sucked deeply on the unlit cigar. His expression was all the answer Meg needed.

'So, what happened?' asked his ghostly partner, forgetting all about her target of one sarcastic remark per sentence.

'The Westgate under-twelves got knocked out of the inter-college championship football final in the semi-finals. The team never got to play in Croke Park. Every boy's dream in those days. So, a group of us snuck out of the dormitory one night and traipsed halfway across town to the playing fields. The team wanted to climb the fence and have a kick around, just to say they'd played in Croke Park. Anyone could tag along, even poor farmers, like me.'

'So, how did you foul up?'

'I climbed up on the fence, no problem. But I just couldn't go down the other side.'

'You chickened out.'

Lowrie was miserable. 'I know, I know. I chickened out. The one time I had the chance ... The only time I was ever asked to join in. I don't know, sometimes even I don't like myself.'

'I suppose none of the other lads would speak to you after that?'

'I wish that was all.'

'Worse?'

'Much worse.'

'Go on. Tell me.'

Lowrie took a breath. 'I was caught climbing down off the fence.'

'Oops.'

'Oops is right. The night watchman called the Brothers and they came over in the van and rounded the boys up like cattle.'

'They weren't happy, I bet.'

'Nope. Mass expulsion. Everyone got kicked out ...'

'Except you.'

'Except me. Not only that, but I was held up as an example for making the sensible decision. Imagine being called sensible in front of four hundred boys at an assembly!'

Meg shuddered. 'Nightmare.'

'No one spoke to me for the rest of the year.

'So now you want to go back.'

'I have to go back. It was a moment when my life could have become completely different. You must have had one of those, Meg. A split second when it all goes wrong?'

In her mind's eye, Meg saw herself outside the granny flats, wondering whether or not to vault through the window.

She nodded. 'I understand. You have to go back.'

Lowrie sighed. 'Thank you.'

'I don't suppose you could just go back during the day and get a guided tour?'

'No. It's the breaking in that's important.'

'I was afraid of that. This is going to play havoc with my aura.'

'Ah sure, what's the problem? With your powers, surely we can handle one fence and a night watchman.'

Meg sniggered. 'Ah here, old timer. I think they might have beefed up the security since World War One.'

'Two.'

'Whatever. Just in, run around and out. Nothing complicated, right?'

Lowrie switched the cigar to the other side of his mouth. 'Nothing complicated. Just in and out. Honest to God.' Lowrie rolled his eyes. 'Sure, why would they have beefed up security? Is not as if anyone's going to rob the grass is it?'

Belch and Elph were in holding cell nine. Customs had no idea what they were, and didn't want to let them through without the go-ahead from the lower-downs. Beelzebub was pulled away from World's Greatest Dictators' benefit, and was none too pleased about it.

Two menials awaited him at the soul depot. Their rugged faces were the fire-blasted black of steam-engine drivers. These boys had generally been densely dangerous in their previous lives, so now they were kept out of harm's way, prising reluctant souls from the tunnel wall. They were generally referred to as winkle pickers.

'What?' he snarled at the customs official.

'Search me,' said the lead winkle picker, perhaps a shade less respectfully than he should have. Beelzebub summarily vaporized him with his trident.

'What?' he said to the new first-in-command.

'Two new arrivals, your worship. Holdin' cell nine.'

'And that concerns me because ...'

'Because they stink, majesty. Somethin' awful. Dunno what it is. Never smelt nothin' like it.'

'I never smelled *anything* like it,' corrected Beelzebub.

'You can smell it from here?'

'No, I ... Never mind. Are they sedated?'

'No need, your honour. Two of 'em are blanky blanky. They can't see or hear nothin'.'

Beelzebub fought the urge to point out the grammar mistake. Once upon a time, centuries ago, he had been private tutor to Attila the Hun.

'So? Tunnel shock. Put them through the blender. Use the residue to power my jacuzzi.'

The customs demon shifted uneasily on his three-toed feet.

'Is there a problem with that?' asked Beelzebub. It was more a warning than a question – a trick all teachers know.

'Well,' stuttered the unfortunate soul scraper, painfully aware that his next words might be his last.

'Well what?' snapped Beelzebub, his patience wearing thin. He wanted to get back to the banquet before Mussolini's famous impressionist routine.

'Well, these two are kinda strange.'

'Strange?'

'The doggy one, he just sits there steamin'. And the little one. He's not like a person at all. The way his head keeps spinnin', and he fizzes in and outta focus. I'd say he's more like sumpin' offa TeeVee.'

Once Beelzebub had translated this from swamp-dwelling, shine-running mumbo-jumbo, he brushed past the winkle picker to the small window in holding cell nine's door.

Belch sat drooling on the bench, while Elph hovered above him, trapped in a speech loop.

'Pure one hundred per cent good,' he buzzed. 'Pure one hundred per cent good.'

Beelzebub licked his fangs. His plan was going awry. If Peter found out about this, there could be repercussions. He slapped his pockets for the mobile phone. Once it had been recovered, he pressed the single dial pad. Saint Peter picked up on the third ring.

'Hey, Amigo. *Que pasa?*'

'What is it, Bub? I'm a busy man.'

Beelzebub searched frantically for someone to vaporize, but the winkle picker had wisely skipped out of range.

'Can't a friend call to say hi?'

'Yes, a friend could. You, on the other hand, are not a friend to anyone except your own miserable self.'

Beelzebub's face was contorted with rage, but his voice remained jovial. 'Hey. Pietro, I'm hurt. After all I've done for you.'

'Do you *have* to speak in tongues, Bub? Why do you people always have to do that? It's so … Hollywood. Insecure, if you ask me.'

One day, gatekeeper, thought Beelzebub. One day. 'Say, listen, Pete. That Irish girl.'

'What about her?'

'Did she ever turn up at the Pearlies?'

'Why? Did your Soul Man come back empty handed?'

'What Soul Man? I'm bleeding here, Peter. Injured.'

'Hrummph,' grunted Peter doubtfully.

'Well, have you seen her?'

There was a long pause. Peter was wrestling with his duty. Saints are not allowed to lie, not even to demons.

'No,' he sighed eventually. 'No sign of her yet.'

Beelzebub grinned. 'Well, I'm sure she'll seal her own fate eventually without any help from us.'

'I'm sure,' grunted Peter, terminating the call.

The demon danced a delighted jig. The game was still on. He walked briskly to the wall-mounted intercom.

'Central?' he said, his mouth brushing the speaker.

'Central here,' replied the voice of an Oscar-winning actress. Oscar winners, the place was packed with them. They parted with their souls nearly as easily as computer programmers.

'This is Number Two.' He hated that code name. Why did the Master insist on it? It was almost as if he wanted his lieutenant to be laughed at.

'Go ahead, Number Two.'

Beelzebub couldn't be sure, but he thought he heard muffled sniggering. 'Get Myishi down to the holding cells.'

'Yes, sir. Right away, sir.'

'Oh, and tell him to bring his tool box.'

The security had been beefed up considerably. A chain-link fence ran the entire perimeter of the stadium, with the exception of the security kiosk and the six-metre gates. Security cameras buzzed and whirred from atop concrete poles.

'Told you,' said Meg, in that teeth-grinding tone children are so proficient at.

Lowrie decided that this would be a good time to light the cigar. 'So, you were right for once. What are you going to do about it?'

'The same as we did with Dessie. Bit of a brain fidget with the guards, then Open Sesame, in we go.'

Lowrie took a long pull on the cigar. The glowing ember lit his face like a rush of blood.

'Nope. That's no good.'

Meg frowned, creasing the ghostly freckles across the bridge of her nose.

'No good? And why's that? Too simple, is it? Or maybe you'd like to give the security guards a kiss too?'

'I have to break in,' explained Lowrie. 'It has to be risky. That's the whole point.'

'I don't know what breaking and entering is going to do to my aura. That's what got me into this mess in the first place.'

'You'll know soon enough. Now let's go!'

Before Meg could protest, Lowrie set off hobbling across the road, his cigar bobbing like a drunken firefly. They followed the fence around to a shadowy area, backing on to a street of terraced houses.

'This is the spot,' gasped Lowrie, a hand clasped over his heart.

'Go on, have another cigar, why don't you?'

The old man fired the butt into the muck, stubbing it out with the heel of his new loafers.

'You're right. No point speeding up the … process.'

'So this is where you went over. Fifty years ago.'

'More.'

From the base, the fence seemed huge. The Mount Everest of fences. Insurmountable. And even if you did somehow manage to scale the heights, there was a friendly closed-circuit camera waiting to immortalize your mug at the top.

Lowrie coughed. It started small, but built to a shuddering crescendo, racking his whole body. He could feel his heart booming in his ears. It reminded him just how sick he was. Meg floated down to his level.

'Are you sure about this, partner?'

Lowrie's coughing trailed off to a rumbling wheeze. 'Sure? Yes. While I still can.'

'OK so. But at least let me take out that camera. In all fairness, they didn't have those before the war.'

Lowrie spat a lump of phlegm on to the grass. 'I suppose so.'

Meg floated to the top of the fence. The metallic camera buzzed at her like an inquisitive robot.

CAMERA, she thought, twisting the lens sharply to the right, film another part of the lane for a while.

From above, Lowrie looked even more pathetic. Even a new suit couldn't disguise the droop in his shoulders, or the shake in his hands. It was obvious, even to a teenager, that he couldn't go on like this. His six months could become weeks, even days, if he kept going at this rate.

'Lowrie, you should be in a hospital,' she said gently, alighting from the fence top.

'No,' snapped the old man, a sheen of cold sweat shining on his forehead. 'What can I do in a bed? The same as I've done all my life. Nothing! Now, are you going to help me or not?'

'I don't know. I don't know if I should.'

'Worried about your precious aura?'

'No. For some stupid reason I was worried about you.'

The pair of them sulked for a while then. Apparently that's an ability you hold on to even when you're dead. Meg had the advantage though, because she couldn't feel the bitter wind swirling up her trouser legs.

'Well?' said Lowrie eventually, disgusted that he'd been first to break the frosty silence.

Meg sighed. 'Move over.'

The possession was easier every time. As though she knew which part of the brain to sit in. No messing about with embarrassing old memories or disgusting bodily functions she wanted nothing to do with. But it was harder too, in a way. Meg could feel her energy waning, it was like being out of breath, but only in your head. (And if you're a spirit reading this, that makes perfect sense.)

She flexed Lowrie's fingers and toes. They were as stiff as rusted gates.

'This is not going to be easy.'

The fence stretched above her, seeming much higher now that she was earthbound. The holes between the links were diamond-shaped and tiny. No way Lowrie's big clodhopping shoes were going to fit in there. She took them off and knotted the laces around her neck. The muck instantly saturated her socks and feet.

'That's cold,' she giggled. 'I remember cold!'

'Will you get on with it!' shouted Lowrie from inside his own head. 'Before you give me pneumonia!'

'All right, grumpy. Keep your hair on!' She patted the crown of Lowrie's head. 'Oops, too late.'

Messing and joking aside, it was a daunting task. Even if Meg had the use of her own teenage body, she wasn't sure if she could do it. She hooked her fingers through the wire and started climbing.

Halfway up, the pain started in her joints. It shot through her limbs like lashes from an invisible whip. And the wind picked up, rattling the links and almost dislodging the fence's grimacing passenger.

'At least it's not rai—'

'Don't say it!' warned Lowrie.

Meg didn't say it. She had never believed in luck, good or bad. But these days she was prepared to believe in absolutely anything. After an age of grunting and sweating, she managed to straddle the top bar.

'You sweat like a pig, old man,' she muttered. 'This shirt is ruined.'

His heart was throbbing too. Her presence wasn't enough to completely pacify it any more. She had no doubt that if Lowrie had attempted that climb on his own, he'd be a corpse in the mud right now.

Meg paused at the top for a short break. The wind buffeted them from all sides. You'd think there'd be a bit of shelter from the massive shadowy stands. But no. The wind weaseled through the gaps, concentrating itself like water from a pipe.

She swung over the other side. Lowrie's legs were next to useless now, so his entire bulk swung from the knuckles. The joints groaned and threatened to pop. After an eternity of struggle, she collapsed to the ground. Puddle water soaked through the seat of Lowrie's trousers. Meg hadn't the energy to care.

'I don't know how we're getting out,' she gasped, 'but it won't be over that fence. Another climb like that would finish off both of us.'

She slipped out of the old man's head, returning control of the body to its owner. Lowrie instantly felt the full impact of his swollen heart hammering in his chest.

'This is madness,' he gasped. 'Stupid.'

For once Meg was glad to be a spirit. At least she'd already been through the whole death thing.

'That's what I said.'

Lowrie lay against the fence for several moments, the shuddering in his chest gradually subsiding to a flat throb.

'OK,' he breathed. 'I'm better now. Let's go on.'

'Are you sure?'

The old man pulled himself to his feet. 'Well, there's no

point giving up now, is there? We've already done the hard bit.'

'We? You just sat there and watched. I was the one dragging your wasted old body over the fence.'

'That's what you're here for, isn't it?'

'Suppose.'

'Good. So could we please stop arguing and get on with it, before I actually do have a heart attack?'

CHAPTER 8: THE EQUALIZER

CROKE Park was well illuminated even at this time of night. Orange lamps buzzed high overhead throwing ominous shadows across the hulking stands. The grounds were littered with bottles and cans; the wind had swept them into corners like garbage drifts. Obviously the grounds crew hadn't yet done the clean-up after a big game.

Lowrie limped on to the pitch itself. Night lights cast a pale wash over the grass, painting it a ghostly white. The old man couldn't stop himself grinning. He was here. Actually here, after all these years. He strode out to the centre circle, arms outstretched, basking in the applause of his absent classmates. Now, yez mockers. Who hasn't the guts? Who's a big farmer chicken?

'It's me!' he shouted, his voice echoing under the Hogan stand. 'It's Lowrie McCall sneaking in at the dead of night!'

Meg giggled, she could see the happiness emanating from the old man like little orange fireworks.

'I'm here to put one over the bar in Croke Park!'

'Are you, now?' said a voice.

The partners turned to look. A security guard was pitching

them a very intolerant look, his radio slung low on his hip like a six-shooter.

'And what I want to know,' he continued laconically, 'is how the pair of ye intend to put one over the bar, when you haven't a football between you?'

Lowrie swallowed. Meg blinked. Two thorny ones there. One: how indeed were they going to play football without a ball? And two: what exactly did the security guard mean by *the pair of ye*?

The guard's fingers flexed, gunslinger style, over his holstered walkie talkie.

'Give me one good reason why I shouldn't —'

Lowrie interrupted his speech. 'Don't I know you?'

It was niggling at Meg too. Something familiar.

The security guard shrugged. 'Don't think so. Anyway, don't be changing the subject. Give me one good —'

'You don't have a brother, by any chance?'

'Dessie?'

'Same business?'

'Security consultant like myself. Guards all the bigwigs over in RTÉ, if you don't mind.'

'With a degree in medieval poetry?'

'Dirty limericks is more like it. Do you know him?'

Lowrie nodded. 'Sort of. He opened the gate for me today.'

'Small world,' the guard extended a hand. 'I'm Murt. Any friend of Dessie's and so on ...'

Lowrie shook the hand hesitantly, on the lookout for a sly handcuffing. Formalities over, Murt was all business again.

'Anyway, back to the matter at hand. Ahem, give me one —' the guard cut himself off this time, realization chasing itself across his face like a galloping virus. 'Hey. Lowrie McCall! You're *him*, aren't you?'

'Him who?'

'Off the telly. Kissing Cicely Ward. You cheeky old monkey.'

'Sorry, wrong man.'

'Go on out of that, of course it was. I'd recognize that wrinkly old mug anywhere. Sure, you've been plastered all over the evening news, with your *olé* and your hopping around like Errol Flynn.'

Lowrie couldn't help a little smug grin. 'OK, it was me.'

'What are you? An escaped lunatic, gallivanting around kissing celebrities?' Murt's eyes widened. 'Here, you're not staking out another victim at this very minute are you?'

'No, it's nothing like that!'

'I hope not. It's one thing getting into these scrapes yourself. It's quite another dragging the young lady with you.'

'What young lady?' said Lowrie innocently.

'Are you trying to be funny?'

'He can see me,' hissed Meg, grateful that she had decided to walk instead of hovering. Who said that sulking never did anyone any good?

'Of course I can see you. Although, funnily enough, I didn't notice you on the camera monitor in the kiosk.'

'There's a camera on the pitch?'

'Well, of course there is. Who'd be stupid enough to think we'd guard the fence and not the pitch? And I didn't notice that girl on the monitor.'

'Well, that's because I'm a —'

'That's because she's always lagging behind,' cut in Lowrie. 'You'd think, now, she'd be able to keep up with an old fossil like me, but no.'

Murt backed off a step. 'Maybe the pair of you are lunatics. I'm going to call this in.'

'No, Murt!' said Lowrie, trying to remain calm. 'Let me tell you why I'm here. The truth. Everything. All about Sissy Ward. The works. A story like that. The Sunday papers would pay a fortune for it.'

Murt chewed the edge of his moustache, considering the deal. 'You reckon? One of those exposés?'

'Exactly.'

'I'll tell you what I'll do. Let's have the story, and then I'll decide.'

'That's not fair!' protested Meg. 'Sure, you're holding all the cards then.'

'Life's not fair, kiddo,' grinned Murt.

'Tell me about it,' muttered the suddenly visible spirit.

'OK. It's a deal,' interrupted Lowrie, before Meg antagonized a possible ally.

'Great,' beamed Murt. 'Go ahead, so. The whole truth and nothing but the truth. My line of work has trained me to spot fairy stories a mile off.'

'The whole truth,' Lowrie whistled.

So, as promised, he told the night watchman exactly what was going on. The truth. Well, a loose interpretation of the truth. OK, a pack of barefaced, baldheaded lies. Lies, he reasoned that would not get them banged up in an insane asylum.

'It all began ... ah ... last Friday week.'

'Really,' commented Meg. 'This should be interesting.'

'When ... ah ... Meg's grandfather was lying on his deathbed.'

Meg sobbed dramatically. 'Poor old Gramps.'

'There we were, all gathered around, waiting for the poor

man's ticker to give out.' When you're telling a lie, always fire in as much of the truth as possible. Lowrie sneaked a peek at Murt to see if his fairy-story detector was picking up anything. The night watchman seemed suitably engrossed in the fabrication.

'Now, Granda was a nice old gent, but sort of useless. His life had flown by and he'd just watched it go. He felt, lying there, that he wasn't much of a role model for his young granddaughter. So he dragged a promise out of me.'

'What sort of promise?' asked Meg, intrigued in spite of herself. 'I mean, yes, he dragged a promise out of old Lowrie here, who used to be ...'

Lowrie winced. Meg's fibs probably wouldn't be as tame as his own.

'Who used to be in his commando unit during the war.'

Murt raised an eyebrow. 'That explains how an old fossil like him could get over the perimeter fence.' The eyebrow settled back into its natural groove. 'So what was this promise?'

Lowrie scratched the spot on his chin where his stubble used to be. 'The promise ... Yes ... It was that I, his best friend –'

'And commanding officer in the Fighting Terriers,' interjected the spook, thoroughly enjoying herself at this stage.

'Yes,' said Lowrie through gritted teeth. 'And commanding officer in the Fighting ...'

'Terriers.'

'Terriers. Thank you, Meg. I promised that I would do all the things that he regretted not doing.'

Murt whistled. 'And one of those things was kissing Cicely Ward.'

'Exactly.'

'And now you want to have a kick about in Croke Park?'

'If possible.'

Murt chewed the tip of his moustache. This was a tricky one. Technically, it was an open-and-shut case. Breaking and entering. No question as to his duty. Get on to the blower to the police and let them handle it. But ...

'Where's your ball, then?'

Meg and Lowrie grinned sheepishly. 'Forgot it.'

'Commandos, how are ye,' snorted Murt. 'God Almighty, I must be going off me rocker. Hang on there one minute.' Murt turned and jogged across to the security kiosk, torch and radio slapping against his leg.

Meg released a giggle that had been bubbling behind her lips for several moments. 'I can't believe he bought it!'

'No thanks to you. The Fighting Terriers!'

'I just thought I'd liven things up a bit.'

'Thanks very much.'

'Welcome.'

The pitch stretched before them, a solitary crisp bag swirling across its surface like a rustling ice skater.

'Sorta spooky really, isn't it?' whispered Meg.

'You're the expert.'

'Seriously, though. Him being able to see me. I wonder why? What's special about him?'

Lowrie shrugged. 'I don't know. Maybe you wronged him too. While you were alive.'

'Don't even know the chap.'

'You never made anonymous phone calls or anything?'

'Not to Dublin. No one ever accepted the charges.'

'We can wonder about this later. You'd better get in here and do your stuff before Murt gets back.'

'I thought you'd want to do this on your own.'

Lowrie chortled. 'I'd love to do it on my own, but ever since two burglars' mutt chewed up my leg, my kicking has gone to the dogs, if you'll pardon the pun.'

'Oh, bring that up again, why don't you,' grumbled Meg, sliding into Lowrie's skin. 'It's been a whole ten minutes since you mentioned that.'

Murt trotted back, his belly jiggling with each step.

'Here you are,' he puffed, lobbing a leather football to Lowrie. The person he thought was Lowrie caught it dextrously, spinning it on one finger like one of those basketball chaps. Meg had been an expert netball player in her day.

'I'm telling you, Murt,' she said. 'You want to get yourself in shape. That spare tyre you're carrying is going to send you up the tunnel before your time.'

Murt jerked a thumb back towards the players' tunnel. 'I've just been up the tunnel. Anyway, where's the girl?'

Lowrie, the spectator in his own head, was instantly flustered, but Meg had a lifetime's experience of quickfire lies behind her. 'She got a call on her mobile,' she explained in Lowrie's gravelly tones. 'She's recording an album at the moment and they need her for emergency backing tracks.'

Murt squinted doubtfully. 'I see. So she's gone back over the fence, is she?'

'Yes. Very athletic, that girl. As a matter a fact, she's on the Irish athletics squad.'

'Right.' Obviously Murt's fairy-story detector wasn't very sensitive.

'Yep. Won two golds at last year's Olympic games.'

'Last year's?' said Murt, trying to divide by four in his head.

'The long run one, and the jumpy one.'

'Marathon and hurdles?'

'That's them. She's such a wonderful kid. I'm thinking of adopting her.'

'I thought it was her granda that had died?'

'Yes ... eh ... but he was also her father, having adopted her when her real parents died in ... a freak baboon attack in a safari park.' Inside in the cranial cinema, Lowrie's consciousness didn't know whether to laugh or cry.

Murt rubbed his temples. He could feel a headache building. 'OK, enough about wonder kid. Are you going to kick this ball or not?'

'Of course I am. That's what I'm here for, isn't it?'

Meg walked out on to the hallowed turf of Croke Park. Residual memories erupted from the stands, urging long-retired teams to victory. All around her, shades of past players dodged, weaved and hacked the legs from under each other when the ref wasn't looking. The excitement was contagious. Meg could almost believe that she was a part of one of those finals. It was her job to convert the winning penalty in the last seconds of the game. She could feel Lowrie's heart pound with excitement. Finally, after fifty years, he was fulfilling a dream.

Meg placed the white leather ball on the turf and took eight steps back. The ghostly crowd fell silent. The players fizzled away, burnt out by the intensity of the moment. Lowrie said a silent prayer. She could do it. He used to be a fair enough footballer in his day. Meg could use his memories. He sent them to her. Every ball he had ever kicked. Every match that he had spent tearing around some mud-mired pitch. It was all there, filed away in a dusty stream of electrons in the back of his head.

'Oh,' said Meg and changed her stance completely. She

angled her shoulders, putting the weight on the back foot. No problem. Barely a breath of wind, and right under the posts.

For the first time, they were truly cooperating. Brain and brawn working together. Meg licked Lowrie's finger and stuck it into the wind. Then the taste of tobacco bit into the tastebuds she was inhabiting.

'Oooh,' she groaned, spitting on to the grass. Of course, being in possession of ancient nicotene-drenched lungs, quite a bit more stuff came up than she was expecting.

'That's disgusting. What are you doing to yourself?'

'Let that be a lesson to you,' Lowrie shouted from his hideaway.

'What? Smoking can seriously damage your health?'

This exchange, though quite typical for the Meg-Lowrie partnership, seemed quite puzzling to poor Murt.

'You're mad, aren't you? An utter nutter. That's what it is. I'm aiding and abetting Mr Looney. I should be locked up meself.' The security guard reached for his radio.

'No, Murt, wait,' shouted Meg desperately. 'It's flash-backs. I'm getting flashback to my days with the Fighting Terriers. Sometimes it all seems so real.' She hitched a crocodile sob, peering between her fingers to see how Murt was reacting.

'Oh, go on, then. I'm telling you, the *Sunday World* had better pay me a fortune for this story after all the grief I've had to put up with.'

Meg took a deep breath and took a run at the ball. She whacked it with her instep, just as Lowrie's memories had shown her. The ball wobbled, bounced and rolled about a metre.

Murt nearly broke his jaw laughing.

'Oh no ...' he howled. 'Oh stop, stop! I'm not able for comedy like that.'

'That ball's hard,' groaned Meg, rubbing Lowrie's stumpy old toe. 'I've only kicked those free plastic ones from the petrol station.'

Murt clapped his hands with sheer glee. 'Are you sure it wasn't the Fighting Poodles you were in?'

'OK, Murt. Very good.'

'I think there's a girl guide's hall nearby. Will I run down and get a few young ladies to show you how to kick?'

Lowrie moaned internally. 'He's right. You kick like a ...'

'Like a what?'

'Well, you know. Like a ...'

'Like a *girl*? Is that it?'

'Well ...'

'I am a girl,' shouted Meg. 'I'm a girl, all right? What did you expect?'

Of course poor old Murt, being a decent sort of a chap, felt bad then. 'You are not a girl. I was only having a laugh. Go on, have another go.'

But Meg wasn't just going to comply straight away. She felt entitled to a good sulk and muttering session. 'Stupid old eejit, with your list, and your oh-help-me-fix-up-my-life. I'm doing my very best. I got you the kiss, didn't I? Nearly got killed, or something. And what do I get? Abuse. You kick like a girl. I've a good mind to head off back up the tunnel right now.'

'Ah, don't go up the tunnel,' said Murt placatingly. 'Have one more lash at it.'

'Why should I?' pouted Meg, forgetting who she was

supposed to be. 'Why should I put myself out for some ungrateful old codger?'

Murt drew himself up to his full height. 'Because that old codger is your best friend. Do it for him, and do it for the little girl. She could do with a role model.'

Amazingly enough, even though he had no clue what was going on, Murt managed to hit the nail on the head.

Wordlessly, Meg retrieved the ball, replacing it on the penalty spot.

Lowrie's voice came whispering from somewhere dark. 'Thank you.'

'Don't thank me yet,' advised Meg, taking eight giant steps backwards. 'That thing is like a rock.'

Murt came in from the sideline, radio slapping against his hip. 'Bit of advice for you.'

'Oh great,' said Meg. What she meant was: go away.

'Whenever I had to kick a ball a fair distance,' Murt continued, blithely unaware of the hostility waves breaking over his forehead, 'I used to imagine it was someone's head. Someone I wasn't too fond of.'

Meg froze. That *was* good advice. Turn the ball into a head. And she knew just the head.

She faced up for the kick. The ball was not an innocent leather sphere anymore, it was Franco's head. And it was talking to her. '*This is my house now, Missy. So there'll be no more spoiling the little princess. You'll do what I say, and when I say it ...*'

'Is that a fact?' said Meg, beginning her run.

'*You can forget your old life for a start. I'm not your maid. I'm not going to be chasing around after you, picking up the laundry. It's a new day, Missy, a brand new day. And your mammy won't be coming back to save you. Because your precious mammy is ...*'

'Shut up!' grunted Meg, kicking the ball harder than she had ever kicked anything in her life, or since.

Franco's head spiralled into the air, smack bang through the uprights and into the crowd-protection net behind. Then it was just a ball again, sliding back to Earth.

Murt was flabbergasted. 'I take it all back,' he breathed. 'The Brownies couldn't teach you a thing. That was one hell of a kick. I haven't seen anything like that since ... well, ever. It nearly cleared the nets, for heaven's sake. I thought it was gong to punch right through.'

Lowrie was dancing a jig inside his own skull. 'I knew you could do it. I knew it. That felt good. That felt great. I feel like a boy again.'

A slow smile spread across Meg's face, or the one she was wearing at that moment. 'You're right,' she said, the memory of Franco's surprised expression fresh in her vision. 'That did feel good.'

Murt escorted his charge out to the turnstile.

'You're not going to get into trouble for this, are you?'

Murt shook his head. 'No. I let you take a kick before throwing you out. Big deal. Anyway, I own the security company.'

Meg nodded. 'Good. Listen, Murt, thanks. It meant a lot to Lowrie ... me, it meant a lot to me.'

'No problem whatsoever. Always glad to help one of the Fighting Terriers.'

And before Meg could react, Murt grabbed Lowrie's hand and began pumping it vigorously. A part of Meg slipped into him before she hurriedly sucked herself back in.

Murt withdrew his hand, studying his fingers curiously. 'Hmm,' he mumbled. 'That was ...'

'That was what?'

Murt blinked. 'Nothing. I just thought … Oh nothing.'

'So bye, Murt. Regards to Dessie.'

'Sure thing. Listen, do you mind if I ask you a question?'

'No, fire ahead.'

'That girl, the Olympian singer?'

'Yes?'

'Are you sure you're not related to her?'

'Positive. Why?'

Murt frowned. 'It's just that … Sometimes when I look at you, I seem to see her face.' He laughed nervously. 'I must be going a bit loopy.'

Meg and Lowrie laughed together, perhaps a decibel too loudly. 'You must be, Murt. You must be.'

The night watchman locked the turnstile behind them, and once again they were on the city streets. As soon as Murt had returned to the shadows of Croke Park, Meg disentangled herself from Lowrie's cell structure.

'Owww,' groaned Lowrie. 'My foot. You must have hit that ball some whack.'

'Hmm,' said Meg glumly.

'Hey!' said Lowrie. 'What's wrong with you? That's two out of four. Halfway there.'

Meg sat on a wall, more out of habit than a need to rest. 'It's Murt. I know why he could see me.'

'Really? Why?'

'Just now, when we shook hands, I got a bit of a look around inside him. It was an accident. I'm not a snoop or anything.'

'No?'

'It's his life force. His energy — whatever you call it.'

'What about it?'

'It's empty. Gone. Used up.'

'He's dying?'

Meg frowned. 'My mam used to say about our car, when we had a car, that the engine was running on fumes. Out of juice. I think Murt's like that. More spirit than flesh. That's why he could see me. I'm one of his own. Nearly.'

'Nothing you could do?'

Meg shook her head. 'No. That sort of thing is beyond me. Well, at least his aura is bright blue. He'll be up at the Pearlies before he knows he's passed on.'

Murt watched them go from the guard tower. He stared wide-eyed as the girl separated herself from the old man. He knew it. He knew there was something odd about that pair. He fumbled a video tape from its packaging, pressing it into the VT slot. Too late. The strange couple had disappeared into the shadows.

This was big. Bigger than he'd thought. And, funnily enough, he felt he understood it. She was a spirit on a mission. Now, how would he know that? Murt shrugged, it was just a theory. No point in getting himself all worked up about it. He should get on to Dessie though, get some advice on how to handle this. Dessie was always the one with the head for business.

Just the thought of listening to one of Dessie's lectures sent his blood pressure rocketing. Before you knew where you were, this would be Dessie's project and he'd be a junior partner. Still, though, his little brother knew how to squeeze a few shillings out of a situation.

You needed fortification before talking to Dessie. A nice strong cup of tea would be the very man. Murt swung himself out of the swivel chair and toddled into the kitchenette. The kettle sat leaking on the draining board. Frayed wires were jammed into a charred-looking plug. He should fix that, really, or go the whole hog and get a new kettle altogether.

Murt shrugged. He'd do it tomorrow. This was a refreshment emergency. Surely the old girl was good for one more brew up? Murt shook a few stray drops of water from the plug, and reached towards the socket ...

Myishi tapped the brain spike's monitor. 'Here's the problem. Right here.'

'About time,' snarled Beelzebub. The whole evening had been a disaster. Just for him, of course. All the other senior demons were busy gorging themselves on endangered species in the red room.

'Everything was going according to plan, no thanks to your Soul Man, I might add, when the old man kisses the old woman, and BANG!'

'BANG? What are you talking about, you technofool?'

Myishi held his breath, swallowing the retort that it was actually Beelzebub himself who was the true technofool. Observations of that nature usually led to a level-four shock in a very painful place.

'You see that white light, Beelzebub-san?'

Hell's Number Two leaned into the monitor. It was quivering slightly in Belch's brain matter. 'Yes. Of course I see it.'

'Good. One hundred per cent positive energy. Very rare. A perfect moment. Not a single deadly sin involved. You get two molecules of goodness bumping into each other like that, and BANG! Molecular fusion. Anathema to our kind. Chewed up your boy like a shark crunching on a baby turtle.'

Beelzebub shuddered.

'Fried his brain, again. Drained his energy, and sent him

back here faster than a hyena ripping meat from a …'

'All right, all right, you horrid little man. I get the picture.'

Myishi smiled a secret smile. Squeamishness. Not exactly an attribute in this part of the cosmos.

'Anything useful on the tape?'

'No, Beelzebub-san. Just static after the kiss.'

'And what about your little robot. Your fairy?'

'That's Elph.'

'Fairy, elf, whatever. Did it record anything useful?'

Elph was still flickering overhead, interminably mouthing the same sentence. Mercifully, Myishi had muted his volume.

'I'm afraid the system crashed after the overload, but I can reboot from the server …' He paused, remembering what had happened the last time he'd buried Beelzebub under a mound of jargon. Sure enough, there was a sizzling charge growing on the tip of his superior's trident. 'I mean the hologram shut down, but I can start it up again.'

'Good. Why didn't you say that in the first place? And can't you do something about the smell? It's revolting.'

Myishi sniffed hesitantly. 'Nothing much. It'll wear off eventually. It's the scent of happiness. Eau de Joi. Not a hint of evil in it. Reminds me of flowers …'

'And baking.'

'And soap.'

'And a breeze from the ocean.'

The demons shivered.

'Disgusting,' they stated simultaneously.

A historic moment. The first and probably last time Beelzebub and Myishi were to agree on anything.

Beelzebub didn't like the feeling. 'So, get them started up again. And none of your repair-shop excuses. The parts do not have to be shipped from Taiwan, so you have ten minutes before I start inflicting serious scorch damage on the seat of your lovely silk suit. Are we clear?'

Myishi bowed deeply. 'Crystal, Beelzebub-san.'

The programmer stripped off his jacket to reveal a torso completely covered in ornate tattoos. Dragons rippled across his chest and tsunamis crashed over his shoulders. Holding his breath against the stench of goodness, Myishi once more plunged into the morass of Belch's grey matter.

Like all intellectuals, he could not resist the impulse to explain the procedure.

'The wave of positive energy overloaded the Soul Man's own life-force reserve. Killed him again, if you like. It also wiped his memory. His head is like an empty bucket. Fortunately, the hologram has a copy of the memory patterns on file. Unfortunately, the hologram operates from the same power source as the host. So one goes down, they all go down.'

Myishi connected the spike to an external power line. A blue spark sizzled down the lead, followed by several others. They leapt into the bowl of Belch's cranium, sending the stupefied Soul Man into spasms. Elph spun like a top, his speech rate increasing to four hundred words a second. His microchips immediately launched a self diagnostic, and the hologram began a thorough check of all drives and programs. Three-point-four seconds later, Elph decided he was eighty-eight per cent functional. His telescopic eyes zoomed into focus.

'Ah, Great One,' he said, executing a low bow.

'Thank you,' replied Beelzebub, flattered in spite of himself. Myishi didn't bother to correct him. 'Is the moron still operational?'

'Arf,' said Belch.

'Regrettably, it would seem so.'

Beelzebub groaned. 'Even your holograms are condescending. Now, Myishi, tell me why I shouldn't fry your fairy friend right now.'

'Allow me to answer,' said Elph, smoothly whirring to his master's side. 'Unlike your Soul Man, my analytical programming, as patented by Myishi Incorporated, Internal Solutions for Infernal Problems, has allowed me to access Mister Brennan's memories, and forecast where our errant soul will appear during her sojourn on the mortal plain.'

Beelzebub glared at Myishi. 'It looks like you, and it talks like you. I hate it.'

Myishi bowed low and repeatedly, all too aware that his digital creation was nanoseconds from a fiery destruction.

'It means, Beelzebub-san, that it knows where Meg Finn will go.'

Beelzebub allowed the full strength of his doubt to show through violet eyes. 'For certain?'

Elph completed some complicated computing.

'According to my host's video feed, the girl is obsessive compulsive. If she believes herself to have unfinished business on Earth, she will attempt to manipulate the old man, so that she may complete it.'

Beelzebub was sold. He wouldn't admit it, but the charge on his trident fizzled out. 'Hmm. And there is, I take it, unfinished business?'

Elph projected a picture of a sullen character on the cell wall. 'Her stepfather. Franco Kelly. Meg Finn harbours strong feelings of resentment towards this man. Despite previous actions she feels there is still a score to settle.'

Beelzebub nodded reluctantly. 'OK. One more chance, but only because I have no choice. This lump of blubber is the only unregistered soul I have. If I could send someone else, anyone else, I would.'

Myishi heaved a relieved sigh. His prototype would survive for another day.

'Since the goodness incident the host's brain capacity is even less than before. I'll juice him up as much as possible, but with all the damage –'

'How long will he have?'

'Twelve hours. Eighteen at the most. After that he'll have to get his life force somewhere else.'

Beelzebub belly butted the oriental programmer against the wall. 'This is *your* last chance too, Myishi. You do know that, don't you?'

Myishi nodded weakly. Funny how your smugness deserted you in the face of oblivion.

'If all your clever technology cannot secure one little soul for the Master, I think we may have to trade you in for a newer model. Upgrade, to use one of your own terms.'

Beelzebub chuckled. He adored turning the tables, in a blackly humorous way, of course. He was, after all, a demon.

Myishi considered muttering some oriental abuse, but thought better of it. Beelzebub could read weak minds; maybe he could speak Japanese too. 'Of course, Beelzebub-san. Most humorous.'

Beelzebub delicately flicked a forked tongue over his fangs. 'I thought so.'

The programmer sighed. He would have to go fiddling around in that hybrid creature's repulsive brain again. It was like asking Michelangelo to work with crayons.

CHAPTER 9: THE SAD BIT

MEG was watching her fingers, or rather she was watching the shimmering aura flickering around them. Red blue, red blue. It still looked purple to her. The intensity was fading though, as her life force diminished. It was getting harder to think HOLE or CHAIR, and hovering wasn't as easy as it used to be. She recalled the words of Flit, the tunnel mite. Time is ticking on, ticky ticky ticky.

'You know what the problem is?' she said to Lowrie, who was doing his best to grab a wink of sleep. An almost impossible task with a forever-alert spirit prowling the room.

'This bed-and-breakfast costs forty pounds a night, you know,' he responded testily, hauling himself up on one elbow.

'So why waste your money sleeping? Stay awake and talk to me.'

Lowrie sighed. She'd left him alone for six hours. He supposed he should be thankful for that much. 'All right. I'm awake. What is it?'

'The problem? Do you want to know what it is?'

Lowrie rolled his eyes. 'Oh, the problem! I'm afraid you'll have to narrow it down a bit for me. The two of us have an inordinate amount of problems, you see. What with me dying shortly, and you being a ghost —'

'No,' Meg interrupted. 'The problem with your list.'

'What about my list?'

'Well. I'm supposed to help you, and this will make my aura turn blue.'

'Right. With you so far.'

'But all the things we're doing, well, they're not exactly legal, so …'

Lowrie nodded. 'I understand. The deeds themselves are counteracting your good intentions.'

'Dead on. My time is running out too. And with you snoring your head off half the time …'

'Us fossils need our rest, you know.'

'I know. I could jump into your head while you're asleep.'

'But that just uses up more energy. It's a heads you lose, tails you lose sort of a situation.' He fished the crumpled Wish List from his jacket pocket, which was drying on the radiator. 'You're not going to like number three, then.'

'Enlighten me. What is it?'

Lowrie took a deep breath. 'It's … eh …' He began patting pockets for his glasses.

'Stop stalling, Lowrie. You wrote the list. Don't tell me you can't remember, all of a sudden.'

Lowrie clicked his fingers. 'Ah! It's come back to me. Number three on Lowrie McCall's Wish List …'

'What?'

'Number three is: Burst Ball.'

Meg nodded. 'What's this one? Let me guess. You burst

one of your soppy friends' football, and now you want to replace it after all these years, and fall sobbing into each other's arms?'

Lowrie shook his head. 'Wrong,' he said, without a trace of humour in his voice. 'There's a man. A vicious bully by the name of Brendan Ball. And I want to punch a hole in his head.'

'Do you want me to go to hell? Is that it?' Meg was furious. Here she was, having just explained her good-intentions-versus-bad-deeds theory, and now the old codger wanted her to assault someone. Not just any someone, but a pensioner! Someone who wouldn't see or hear it coming. She'd be damned for sure. One punch and her aura would turn red faster than a lobster in a pot.

'Don't worry. The last one is totally legal, and moral.'

But Meg was not to be placated. 'The last one! I'll never make it past *this* one. As soon as your knuckles touch this chap's chin I'll be off, zooming down the red hole with a pitchfork hanging out of my backside!'

'Listen, if you were sent back to do this, then this must be the right thing to do.'

Meg paused for a second to compute that statement. 'Easy for you to say. Your immortal soul is not on the line.'

Lowrie sighed. 'Meg, please.'

She searched his face. Honesty and decency fluttered from it like albino butterflies. Meg made a decision then, based on a hunch. One she would keep to herself, but would drag out later for a big 'I told you so' session, if it proved accurate.

'OK,' she smirked. 'I'll do it.'

Lowrie was instantly wary. 'Are you sure?'

'Of course. I said I'd do it, didn't I?'

'Hmmm,' grunted Lowrie suspiciously. But he had learned that where his spooky partner was concerned, you took your victories where you could.

They checked out of the bed-and-breakfast on Leeson Street, hopping on a bus to Heuston Station. Well, maybe 'hopping' is the wrong verb. More of a hobble really, considering the state of Lowrie's kicking foot. Meg wasn't her usually floaty self either, deciding to walk in order to conserve what was left of her energy.

The bus was packed, and as much as Lowrie put on the pathetic old-man face, he looked too suave in the new suit for anyone to offer him a seat. He got recognized too. A grinning grandma, sporting a shocking-purple bouffant hairstyle, detached herself from a group of giggling buddies and barrelled down the centre aisle.

'It's you, isn't it?'

A bit of a strange question. No option but to admit it. 'Yes. It's me.'

The woman turned and shouted down the length of the bus. It was a roar that would have done a sergeant major proud. 'It's him, all right, girls. Didn't I tell you?'

'Go on, Flor,' one shouted back. 'Go for it!'

She turned her attention back to a suddenly nervous Lowrie. 'Well, are you going to kiss me?'

Lowrie swallowed. 'I wasn't planning on it, madam.'

'Oh, do you hear him, with his "madam". Yer a real smoothie. Like that fellow Sean Connery. Only ugly.'

'Thank you,' responded Lowrie uncertainly.

'So, how about it? Isn't that what you do? Run around the place kissing mature women?' Flor closed her eyes, puckering glossy pink lips.

Meg giggled. 'Go on.'

Lowrie shot her a desperate glare. 'Help,' he mouthed silently.

He was saved by the bus driver. 'Heuston Station,' he shouted, opening the pneumatic doors.

Lowrie slipped through the rear exit.

'My stop, madam,' he called from the safety of the street. 'Till we meet again. *Adieu!*'

The bit of French was a great success. Flor flattened her face against the bus window, leaving sloppy lip marks on the glass. Lowrie hid a grimace behind a grin, waving at the departing vehicle.

'Who was that?' asked Meg.

'I don't know, some stranger.'

'Not her. That man with the "madams" and the *adieus.*'

'What are you talking about?' snapped Lowrie, ignoring the puzzled glances from passers by.

'Well,' continued Meg, 'the Lowrie McCall I know doesn't carry on with any of that romantic stuff. He's too busy being a grumpy old coot feeling sorry for himself.'

Lowrie felt a grin coming on and fought hard to contain it. No luck, teeth forced their way out.

'Is that a smile? I might pass out with the shock.'

'Oh, shut up. Sorry — not you, sir,' he explained to a passerby.

In spite of his harsh words, the smile would not go away. Meg was right. He was changing — into his new self. The person he might have been.

There were no empty carriages on the southbound train. A race meeting in Wexford town, apparently. So the partners were forced to suspend communications. That is, Lowrie was forced to keep his mouth shut.

Meg couldn't handle it. Just sitting and not talking. She was a teenager, after all. One of the MTV generation. She needed entertainment.

'Think about it,' she hissed.

Lowrie raised an eyebrow. What?

'That chap. The bully. Think about him.'

Lowrie placed two hands protectively over his ears.

'Don't worry. I'm not going to go fiddling with your brain. But I can already see most of your thoughts, sort of. Like a telly with rubbish reception. But if you think really hard …'

Lowrie closed his eyes and concentrated. A wispy picture swirled and solidified over his head. It was Cicely Ward.

'Not her, Romeo. You have a one-track mind, don't you?'

Lowrie grinned apologetically. He tried again.

Another picture appeared. It was grim with bad recollections. Peripheral objects changed or morphed into one another. But the people were solid. Crystal clear. Those memories were sharp as a knife.

It was a strange way to be told a story, through the eyes instead of the voice of the storyteller. Like a movie about the cameraman, but Meg soon got used to it. She sat entranced, absorbed by this formative episode in the young Lowrie McCall's life. If she had been looking at Lowrie's face instead of over it, she would have noticed the stress lines creasing his forehead. This story was not an easy one for him to tell. But once he'd begun, it rolled out of his brain like it had happened yesterday …

By the time I hit fifteen, I'd toughened up a bit. Country chaps didn't survive in Westgate without developing a thick skin. Either that or getting carted off home, drooling. Sod

Kelly went that way, and Mikser French. Two hardy farmers reduced to sobbing wrecks by years of bullying. No one ever touched them, mind, but there are other ways of bullying. Sly ways.

I'd always been told that bullies were an ignorant bunch. Big sacks of dung with turnips for heads. I found out that wasn't the case. Your townie variety considered himself a sophisticated wit, using savage sarcasm and public humiliation to keep the country bumpkins in their place.

Brendan Ball was a prime example. Anyone else with the surname Ball would have had a nickname – Oddball, for example. But not Brendan. He was too popular to have a nickname. And too dangerous.

For some reason, Ball decided to take a special interest in me. Perhaps my survival of the Croke Park disaster irked him. He had lost several friends in the mass expulsion. Not that he played football himself. Too sweaty. He'd much prefer to stand on the sidelines passing snide comments.

For years I put up with it. Kept my head down and walked on by. Words I told myself, it was only words. I could live with that. Then I hit a spurt. Fifteen, and up I shot like a weed. I was looking *at* Ball's nose instead of up it.

Things began to change for me. The Brothers forgot all about their grudge when I started lobbing points over the bar in the inter-college league. And when Ball shot his comments at me on his way past, they began to bounce off me like skinny fullbacks.

That could have been it. But I got cocky. One thing fate can't tolerate.

I was heading down to the lockers one afternoon, hopping a ball on my foot. You can guess who was coming up the hall against me. Ball and Co. A few recent wins had given the old confidence a boost. So I didn't sidle over to the wall, and I didn't lower my gaze. I gave the lot of them my best grin, spinning the leather football in my hands.

Ball didn't like it. To him, it was like a hound rearing up on its master. He wasn't sure what to do, but with the lapdogs panting at his heels, he had no option but to pass his tired comment.

'Two down, farmer boy,' he said. 'Two down and one to go.'

I realized at that moment that Ball was uncertain. I'd seen the look before on the sports field. In the eyes of goalkeepers who don't know whether to come out or stick on the line.

So I pretended to throw the ball at him. The sort of thing you do a million times a day with your friends. But Ball was no friend of mine. I pretended to throw the ball. And he flinched.

So what? Big deal you might think. And you'd be right. But not for Ball. This was a huge deal. In his short, pampered life, this was probably the worst thing that had ever happened to him. Being caught off guard by a culchie.

I'd say it took about two days for the fire on his cheeks to turn to ice. Then he started plotting.

I, like an eejit, thought that I'd stood up to the bully and he'd never bother me again. Stupid. Stupid. Stupid.

The Westgate College grounds stretched down past the football fields, through a wide meadow and down to the Liffey. Every summer a farmer came in with a bailer and for a modest sum was allowed to cart off the hay.

Of course it was forbidden to venture down to the river after dark. Except for one week after exams in June. For those few days, it was an unwritten law that the seniors could convene on the riverbank for a twilight smoke. Seniors only. Technically illegal. But overlooked.

I should never have ventured down. My only allies, the football team, were overnighting in Roscommon after a friendly. I should have stayed in the dorm, nursing the torn shoulder ligaments that had kept me off the pitch, and counted the hours to home.

But it would only be boarders down at the bank, I reasoned. Ball and his bunch would be safe at home with their mummies. So, I tightened the bandage around my shoulder, gave my hair a lick of the brush and strolled down across the meadow.

I tramped down in shirtsleeves, a thick Aran sweater knotted about my waist. The knot was as big as a football. I remember that jumper. It was a target for the townies. According to them my mother had cornered some innocent sheep and dragged it out of its coat by the hooves.

The boys were flaked out on the bank, blowing smoke into the blue night, or firing stones into the middle of the river. I settled in with the bunch raking a handful of pebbles from the riverbank. It seems tame enough these days, with all the entertainment young people have. But to us, sitting on a riverbank, with rock 'n' roll music floating across from the city, and no work to do — it was the height of luxury.

Then Ball arrived. And, of course, Brendan never travelled alone. His fawning hyenas were hovering like planets around the sun. They shouldn't have been here. Day boys sneaking in was as illegal as boarders sneaking out. But Ball had a score to settle, and so they had forged the river at an upstream dam.

I put my head in my hands and hoped. Maybe they had another reason for returning to the grounds. After all, what had I done? Nothing. Just pretended to throw a ball.

I felt them stop before me. Their sniggers petered out as

they waited for the festivities to begin. Whatever was going to happen, it would be big. Ball didn't get his shoes wet for just any old bullying session.

Brendan, of course, broke the silence.

'Good evening, Mr McCall. And how are things among the farming community?'

Boys didn't often use words like 'community'. They felt strange in our mouths. But Ball did. He spoke like one of those fellows reading the news at the pictures.

I didn't answer. It wasn't a real question. I knew that whatever I said would give him an excuse to start on me.

He kicked my foot. 'Well? How's life in your squalid little cave?'

I didn't even know what squalid meant. But I remember the word all the same.

'Has your mother stripped any more sheep?'

That got a good giggle all round. Stripping sheep. Har de har har. Still, I had to speak then. A chap can't have anyone going on about his mam. I decided to stand up to give me a better chance of escape, or attack.

'I'm not a farmer, Ball. We don't live in a cave, and my mother does not strip sheep.'

'Oh really? Is that a fact now?'

'Yes.'

They were gathered in a semicircle. Eyes bright, even in the shadow of the trees. I realized then that they'd been drinking. I'd seen this look before, at home in Newford. We had a town drunk, the same as every other village in Ireland. Our particular version always decided to settle old scores when he'd had a few. It looked like the same idea had a hold on Ball.

'The thing is, McCall, that I don't care about your exact circumstances. A culchie is a culchie is a culchie.'

I was supposed to reply to that, even though it wasn't a question. Trading insults is like a game of tennis, and Brendan had whacked the ball into my side of the court. The thing was, I didn't want to play. I decided to try the staring-out tactic that was so effective on the football pitch. The thing about that tactic is that on the field, things are more or less even. Here, I was outnumbered ten to one. Me giving Ball the evil eye just made him angrier.

'What's wrong, farmer? Cat got your tongue? Or a sheep maybe, or a cow?'

I ground my teeth. Whatever I said, he would just twist it to make me look stupid.

'Thing is, McCall, you've been getting a bit cheeky lately. Uppity. Not as subservient as you should be.'

Subservient? What self-respecting teenager would use a word like that?

A group of girls had assembled at the opposite bank. They were hanging over the railing, giggling and waving. Ball waved back jauntily. Another wing of his fan club. Here to witness the humiliation of the scholarship boy.

'So from now on,' he continued in a slightly louder voice, so his words would carry, 'I would like you to call me Sir.'

A disbelieving snort shot down my nose. I'd been concentrating so hard on the mouth that I'd forgotten about the nose.

Ball's face burned. 'Is there a problem, bucko?'

I didn't move a muscle. Not even an eyelid.

'I said, is there a problem?'

I chanced a shrug. Neither yes nor no.

Brendan chose to take it as a yes. 'Good. Let's hear it, then.'

I blinked. This had gone far enough.

'Just say: That's fine by me, Sir.'

Stupidly, I chose that moment to speak. 'There's no need for you to call me Sir, Brendan.'

Crickets had been sawing in the trees, but I'd swear even they shut up at that moment. The silence didn't last long. The downside to being a bully is that even your friends secretly long for your downfall. The girls at the fence laughed hysterically, slapping the bars with glee.

'Good lad, Paddy! You tell that big bully.'

I guessed that I was Paddy. Brendan guessed it too, and made the transformation from sophisticated wit to thug in the blink of an eye.

Before he knew what he was doing, he lashed out with his hand. The fingers caught me across the mouth. It was stingy, but no big deal. I'd had worse slaps from a fish's tail. Ball gazed in surprise at his fist, as though it had betrayed him. He'd blown his cool, and in public.

Taking advantage of confusion is a footballer's favourite strategy, so that's what I decided to do. I planted my palms in that loudmouth's chest and pushed as hard as I could. He keeled over and slid down the bank on his backside. Most embarrassing.

Ball's gang was on me quicker than hounds on a fox. They were weak enough, never having done a day's work in their lives. But there were a lot of them and they pinned me to the slopes, mud squelching around my ears.

The girls were still laughing on the fence. We were like theatre to them, like a serial at the cinema.

Ball climbed back up the slope, slapping the mud from his blazer. He didn't look happy.

'Ask me to let you go,' he said, swallowing his anger before the audience.

'What?'

'You want to get up?'

I nodded warily.

'All you have to do is ask.'

What was he up to now?

'All right. Let me up.'

Brendan shook his head. 'Ah no. No, no. You have to ask properly.'

'Please let me up.'

'No, farmer boy. Properly. Call me Sir.'

So that was it. He was still sticking to the original plan.

'Get stuffed, Ball.'

You could almost see the confusion spinning around his head. Brendan had gotten his own way for the last sixteen years. And here was some farmer standing up to him, metaphorically speaking. And in front of the girls. He placed a dripping shoe on my chest.

'Say it, McCall!'

'You'll be deep in your cold grave, Ball.'

That was a good one. My mother always said that when Dad asked her to bring in the coal.

'I'm warning you, McCall. We'll give you the thrashing of your life.'

I laughed. I couldn't help it. These boys weren't going to thrash anybody. Not enough to scare anyone from a Christian Brother college.

Ball saw it in my face. He knew I wasn't worried about a few punches. A new strategy was called for. He leaned down, his mouth close to my ear.

'Here's what we'll do, farmer boy. Either you call me Sir right now, or we take off your trousers and throw you in the river.'

I nearly laughed again, but then I remembered the girls.

Hanging on the railing, dying for some amusement. Even the thought made me blush.

They had me. Ball sniffed victory.

'It's up to you. Personally I hope you refuse.'

It's different for country chaps. It was then anyway. We didn't know girls. We didn't have the Dubliners' easy way with them. I'd have been mortified to have to dance with one, never mind slosh around a river in my underwear.

'Let me up, Ball,' I grunted. I tried for threatening, but all I managed was borderline desperate.

'Let me up – *what*?'

I sighed. Which was worse? The word or the river? I chose. The wrong choice, I think now, and have thought for fifty years.

'Let me up – Sir.'

And the sound of their laughter still echoes inside my head.

The image above Lowrie's head dissolved in a cloud of coloured light.

'Did you ever think about just getting on with your life?' asked Meg. 'Forgive and forget, that sort of thing.'

Lowrie's lip stuck out like an infant's. He'd been nursing this particular grudge for fifty-three years, and wasn't about to give up on it now.

'It's ages ago, for God's sake. Before loads of stuff was even invented.'

Lowrie didn't answer. He couldn't, with all the other passengers on the train. He didn't have to. Meg didn't need her limited telepathy to read the message shooting from his eyes.

'OK, OK,' she sighed. 'I'll shut up and do what I'm told.

But I'd just like to register an official complaint, in case there's anyone listening upstairs. I do not agree with flattening old people, and I'm only following orders.'

She could see it was working. Lowrie was growing uncomfortable with his own wish. But he wouldn't give in. Not just yet. No problem. She had hours of nagging left in her.

CHAPTER 10: **BURST BALL**

THEY rode the train right to the ferry port of Rosslare. Twelve months a year, the small town was hopping with Americans looking for their roots, Dutch tourists looking for hills and New Age mystics searching for leprechauns. In this company, a man talking to himself seemed the epitome of normality.

'We could have come here first, you know,' complained Meg. 'It's only down the road from Newford – where you live, in case you've forgotten.'

'I know,' replied Lowrie. 'I prioritized the list. In case I ...'

'In case you what?'

'In case I, you know, didn't make it.'

'Oh.'

They walked in silence for a while. Then Meg had a thought.

'How do you know where this chap lives? Have you been stalking him or something?'

Lowrie shook his head. 'No. Dear old Brendan had his face in the local paper a few years ago. He retired down here after an illustrious career in the city. Bought a famous cottage. Used to belong to James Joyce's grandmother.'

'What does "illustrious" mean?'

'That doesn't matter. You know all you have to.'

Meg tutted. 'That other Lowrie didn't last long. Where are all the *adieu*s and the madams now?'

'I'm sorry,' apologized the old man. 'Just thinking about that man sets my blood boiling.'

'I know the feeling,' said Meg, seeing Franco's face in her mind's eye. Now, there was a head that needed punching.

They made their way to the outskirts of the village, past an almost interminable line of bed-and-breakfasts. The afternoon sun was making a watery effort to burst through grey rolls of cloud. Perched atop a hill, like the *Psycho* motel, was Ball's cottage.

'Spooky,' muttered Meg, shivering.

'Spooky?' chuckled Lowrie. 'What sort of ghost are you?'

'One who's not happy bopping old geezers.'

Meg decided to turn the screws a bit. 'Would you prefer a straight nosebreaker? Or maybe a few kicks in the kidneys when he's down?'

'I don't care.'

'What about a headlock till he begs for mercy?'

Two red spots were rising in Lowrie's cheeks. 'I'll leave that to you, will I? You being the expert on matters criminal.'

Meg swallowed a grin. All according to plan.

There were crazy-paving steps running up to the cottage. Lowrie was taking his time mounting the slabs. A slick layer of sweat shone through his sparsely covered scalp.

'Second thoughts?' enquired Meg innocently.

Lowrie rubbed salty beads from the creases around his eyes. 'No. No second thoughts.'

'Sure?'

'Certain!'

Lowrie took a shaky breath and forced himself to calm down. It'd be an awful shame to have a heart attack right here on Ball's doorstep.

'Listen, Meg,' he said. 'Here's my idea. I go in, introduce myself, remind him of that day in Westgate and ask him to call me Sir. When he refuses, as I'm certain he will, then you take over my body and let him have it right on the snobby upper-class jaw.'

'Ten-four, captain. I just hope I don't kill him.'

Lowrie started. 'Kill him?'

'You never know. I don't know my own strength, these days.'

'I don't want you to kill anyone.'

'What? After what he did to you? It's the least I could do.'

Lowrie stopped climbing. 'Don't mess around. A little punch on the chin. That's all I want. No killing, maiming or strokes.'

'I'll do my best. No promises, mind.'

Lowrie continued up the path, his step slightly less determined than usual. A maelstrom of emotions clouded his aura. Fear and doubt spliced with hate and regret. A powerful concoction.

The door was aluminium. Out of place in the salt-weathered brickwork.

'That's typical Ball,' muttered Lowrie. 'The old door probably wasn't good enough for him.'

'Are you going to spend all day admiring the architecture, or are we going to get this over with?'

Lowrie flexed his fingers, reluctant to ring the bell.

'Well?'

'OK, OK. This isn't easy for me.'

Meg knew exactly what he meant. Facing your demons was no picnic. Especially if your demons seemed to be half-human, half-hound from hell.

Lowrie reached up a shaky finger.

'All right, you old fool,' he admonished himself. 'He's just a man. Just a man.'

Then the door opened. Lowrie jerked backwards guiltily, almost tumbling head-over-heels down the crazy-paving steps.

'Very elegant,' muttered Meg.

Brendan Ball stood, shaded by the door frame.

'Yes?' he inquired hesitantly. 'Who is it?'

Lowrie worked up his courage, swallowing half a century's bile. Tell him, go on, tell him!

He never got the chance. His old adversary placed a pair of wire-rimmed spectacles over rheumy eyes.

'My God. It can't be! Lowrie McCall.'

Lowrie nodded, unwilling to trust his voice.

'I don't believe it. Lowrie McCall. Well, come in, for heaven's sake.'

Ball bustled down the hallway, gesturing over his shoulder for Lowrie to follow.

'Oh, he's a real pig,' commented Meg. 'Asking you in like that. The nerve of some people.'

Lowrie aimed one of his vitriolic orange gazes at Meg's head, and followed Ball into the house. They emerged in a sitting room. All polished wood and glass.

'Can you believe it?' said Ball, pointing at the television screen. 'I was just watching you on video.'

Lowrie's head was freeze-framed on the monitor.

'Well, sit down, sit down. Now what can I get you?'

Lowrie sank into an antique leather-trimmed armchair. If Ball hadn't invited him to sit, his legs probably would have given out anyway.

'I'd like a … glass of water, if you have it.'

Ball clapped his hands delightedly. 'Of course, old buddy, of course.'

Lowrie blinked. Old buddy?

'Be with you in a tick.'

And Ball was gone, darting off into the kitchen, like some slightly arthritic whirlwind.

'*I'd like a glass of water if you have it,*' mimicked Meg. 'What sort of revenge visit is this?'

'He's taken me by surprise, that's all,' spluttered Lowrie.

'You were expecting a sixteen-year-old, I suppose?'

'No, of course not. I was expecting …'

Lowrie paused. His ghostly partner was right. He had been expecting a sixteen-year-old. Maybe not the face and body, but certainly the attitude. He'd never for one second dreamed that he'd be recognized, never mind invited in.

Ball swept back into the room. A tray of cakes balanced on a jug of iced water.

'Mr Ball …' began Lowrie.

'No! Not another word until you've refreshed yourself. Your face is the colour of a beetroot, and at our age you have to be careful about these things.' Ball patted his own chest. 'Believe me, I know.'

Lowrie nodded, gratefully accepting a crystal tumbler of water. He drained the entire glass before speaking again. 'Heart trouble?'

Ball nodded. 'Triple bypass last year. Nearly shuffled off the mortal coil. One hell of a wake-up call.'

'Tell me about it.'

'You too?'

'Afraid so. I need a donor. But I'm at the bottom of a list.'

Ball seemed genuinely saddened. 'Oh, but that's terrible. Perhaps I could make a few phone calls?'

Lowrie shook his head. 'No, thank you … eh …'

'Brendan.'

'No, thank you, Brendan. There are four AB negatives waiting in Ireland. The other three are young people.'

'I see.'

Both men were silent for a moment. Heart disease was a real conversation stopper.

'I'm glad you called, Lowrie,' said Ball eventually. 'I've been meaning to look you up, actually.'

'Really?'

'Yes, really.' The old man took a deep breath. 'Since the operation, I've been thinking. About a lot of things. About the past.'

Lowrie was stunned. This was too much. Ball was like him. Just like him. Could they both have changed so much?

'There are a lot of things I regret not doing,' he stared fixedly at the floor. 'And things I regret doing.' Ball ran a thin finger around the rim of his glass.

'Things have been bothering me, Lowrie. Things I have to make amends for.'

'Brendan, there's no need …'

'No, Lowrie, please hear me out. I made myself a promise, lying there in the Blackrock Clinic, that if I ever got on my feet again, there were a few people I'd have to talk to. You were one of them.'

There was a word for this, thought Lowrie. Synchronicity.

'Something happened a long time ago,' continued Ball. 'You probably don't even remember it.'

'I wouldn't bet on it,' muttered Meg, but Lowrie was so engrossed that he barely heard her.

'In my younger days, I was incorrigible. I know we had great times and that you tend to forget the bad times, but there were bad times too.'

Lowrie nodded. They hadn't been erased for him.

'I remember one summer's night. Our final year, when I … grievously embarrassed you in front of a crowd. Made you call me Sir. You have no idea how many nights that terrible act has come back to haunt me. I lie awake cringing at the memory. Can you ever forgive me?'

'Now?' asked Meg. 'Do I let him have it now?'

'No!' blurted Lowrie.

Ball nodded, crestfallen. 'I understand. No need to explain.'

'No, Brendan, I mean — there's no need for forgiveness. It was a lifetime ago. I barely even remember it.'

'Oh, you fibber,' chuckled Meg.

'It's good of you to say that, Lowrie. But we both know how terrible that night was.'

Lowrie sighed. 'Yes, Brendan. You're right. I do remember. It was a terrible night. I often think it affected my entire life.'

'I knew it,' said Ball, dropping his head into shaking hands. 'You had every right to seek me out. Take whatever revenge you will — I have no right to object.'

Lowrie placed a hand on his shoulder. 'That's not why I'm here. That incident really was nothing. And if it affected me for so long, it's because I allowed it to. I only came to look up an old … friend. Nothing more.'

Ball peered out from between his fingers. 'Really?'

'Really. We were children. Children do stupid, cruel things. Consider yourself forgiven and let's have a drink.'

Ball rose from his chair and hugged Lowrie spontaneously.

If Lowrie hadn't already been sitting down, the shock would have dropped him. 'Thank you, old friend.' He disappeared into the kitchen again, a genuine smile tugging at his lips.

'I knew it,' gloated Meg.

'You knew what?'

'I knew you wouldn't hit him.'

'You knew?'

'Yes, I knew! You're too nice. Too decent. No one with an aura as sky blue as yours could go around bopping people.'

'Well, you saw him,' said Lowrie. 'He was sorry. Genuinely sorry. I couldn't hit him. It wouldn't be right.'

Ball returned with a bottle of brandy and two tumblers. 'We shouldn't, you know. Not with our tickers.'

'I know. But once in a while. What the hell! How often do you have a school reunion?'

Ball sat down, serious again for a moment. 'Do you know, Lowrie, when I was in hospital, I didn't have one visitor. Six weeks and no visitors. Can you imagine how lonely that feels?'

Lowrie thought back to his own granny flat and the years of afternoon television.

'Yes, Brendan,' he replied, taking a deep swig of the burning liquid. 'I can.'

CHAPTER 11: A SPARE WİSH

FRAПCO Kelly had solved the broken remote problem. Not that the television's remote control was actually broken, but it might as well be for all the chance there was of Franco dipping into his cigarette money for new batteries.

Anyway, he'd solved the remote problem. The problem being: what do you do when your remote's packed in, and you want to change channels?

You could get up out of the armchair. But that was a bit extreme. Bad enough that you had to raise yourself for food and toilet breaks, without exerting yourself every time the advertisements came on.

You could befriend some local kid and get him to lie in front of the set. But kids these days were notoriously unreliable, and their parents had an annoying habit of wanting them back around news time, just when Franco needed channels changing the most.

Franco reluctantly decided that it was up to him. He would have to rise above his distaste for mental exercise and devise a plan. Something ingenious to dazzle his critics. Couch potato am I? he thought. I'll show them.

His first thought was to use his toes. But they were pudgy and inaccurate. Plus sometimes the sweat caused the buttons to stick. Back to the drawing board.

The second idea was a masterpiece of simplicity. Franco dragged the armchair over to the television. Close to perfect, but there were bugs. Placing the screen directly in front of him meant that he still had to lean forward to manipulate the now slightly pongy buttons. Placing it to the side caused a shift in his viewing position and a resultant pain in the neck muscles. Such a conundrum. Was he to be denied his only pleasure?

At last, with a craftiness born of thirty years a-dossing, Franco hit upon the solution. He lumbered up to the bedroom and wrenched the wardrobe's door from its hinges. Propping the mirrored side before the chair, he angled it slightly to reflect the television screen at his side. Ingenious.

Not only were the speakers now playing directly into his good ear, but the convex nature of the mirror meant that for all intents and purposes he now had a twenty-eight-inch screen. Ah bliss. Now, if only he had a potty …

He wouldn't have to suffer at all if it wasn't for those Finn women. Dead, the cheek of them. Two in one year. What were the chances of that? How was a man supposed to look after himself with no women to order about?

Franco didn't mind them being dead as such. He didn't miss them as people. But he missed their service. Not that the young one had been much good. She hadn't given anything but cheek. But the mother. What a cook. A good little worker too. Twelve hours in the video shop and then home to make the dinner. None of your microwave rubbish either. Oh no. Franco insisted that everything be made from scratch. Then she had to go and walk out under a taxi, didn't she? Just when his back was starting to play up too. Some people have no consideration.

Elph was not impressed.

'I had thought you were on the bottom rung of the evolutionary ladder,' he commented dryly. 'I can see now that I was mistaken.'

'Woof,' said Belch, who was still a bit punch-drunk from the pure-goodness episode. It seemed that his homo sapiens genes had taken the brunt of the explosion and he was more hound than human now.

'This place is such a hovel,' muttered Elph distastefully. 'The kind of place I would expect to find ... well, someone like you actually.'

'Shut up!' snarled Belch, swallowing the urge to rip the hologram pixel from pixel. 'Tell me what I have to do.'

Elph flitted above Franco's armchair.

'This,' he said, pointing a 3D finger at Kelly's greasy head. 'Is your last chance. A psychological profile of the target soul indicates obsessive tendencies ...'

Belch licked a newly sprouted canine. Ectoplasmic slobber dripped from his lips.

Elph noted the new developments. Perhaps I should, as they say, dumb it down, he thought. 'There is a strong possibility that Meg Finn will show up here.'

Belch nodded. It made sense. Meg hated Franco more than anything. Given the chance, she'd be back to settle the score. 'So. What do we do?'

Elph's electronic lip wrinkled in disgust. 'We wait. We wait, and try to ignore the smell.'

*

'Hee hee,' said Lowrie. 'Ha ha, hic.'

'You're drunk!' giggled Meg. It was good to giggle. There hadn't been much to laugh about since the gas explosion.

'No, no,' responded Lowrie, waving a shaky finger. 'Not drunk as such. Tipsy. Different thing entirely.'

They were travelling by rail again. Northbound towards Dublin. The other passengers gave Lowrie a wide berth. The old man was obviously inebriated. There was a distinct smell of alcohol, and he was talking to himself, for heaven's sake!

Needless to say, Lowrie had not utilized Meg's otherworldly strength to bash Brendan Ball. Quite the opposite, in fact, he had ignored Meg altogether and proceeded to polish off half a bottle of brandy with his old classmate. They parted the best of friends, promising to meet again and soon. Lowrie would never have made a promise like that sober. Not when he knew he couldn't keep it.

'That means we have a spare wish,' said Meg.

'Hmm?' mumbled Lowrie. He could have said: what do you mean by that? But it was too much effort.

'Well, I didn't punch anyone, so we have a wish left over.'

''S true. Wish left over.' That sounded lyrical, so Lowrie made it into a song. 'We have a wish left oooooover.'

Meg wasn't laughing now. Something had occurred to her.

'Can I have the wish, then?'

'Hmm?'

'Give me the wish. There's someone I'd like to punch in the face.'

Lowrie's eyes narrowed craftily.

'I know,' he said pointing an accusing finger. 'I know what you want to do.'

'Is that a fact?'

'Yep. 'S a fact. You want to punch Franco.'

'OK, so you know. Now, how about it?'

'Go ahead. Punch him. I'm not stopping you.'

Meg scowled. 'I can't. I've tried, but I can only go where you go.'

Lowrie thought about it. Or rather he tried to think, wading through the fog enveloping his brain. At last he arrived at a conclusion.

'OK,' he pronounced. 'On one condition …'

'What?' asked Meg, even though she already knew what that condition was.

'I want to know what he did,' said Lowrie, suddenly sounding very sober indeed. 'I want to know what he did to make you do that to him.'

Meg sighed. She'd never talked about this. Not to anyone.

'I can't,' she said finally. 'I just can't.'

'Couldn't you just show me?' asked Lowrie, tapping his head.

Meg chewed her lip. 'Maybe. But with your weak heart …'

'I'll risk it.'

'OK. But don't come chasing after me in the afterlife if you have a heart attack.'

Lowrie smiled weakly. 'I won't.'

Meg rolled up the sleeve of her jacket, plunging her hand into Lowrie's ear.

Lowrie giggled. 'That tickles!'

'Stop fidgeting, would you? You might get brain damage or something!'

He stopped fidgeting.

'Right. There we are.'

Lowrie paled. He was being chased by a group of angry rugby players with girly shirts.

'Oops. Wrong memory.'

Meg closed her eyes and concentrated. Think about that day, she told herself. Let it all come back to you. I'm twelve years old plus one day. I've stayed out as long as I can, but it's cold and I'm hungry and there's nowhere else to go ...

I remember sitting in the back of Videovision for hours watching a film on the big monitor. Trish asked me to leave when the evening crowds started coming in. Nicely though. Because she knew Franco. Knew what I had to go home to.

'Sorry, Meggy,' she said. 'You know the drill. The boss-man will be checking in any minute.'

I got up off the windowsill. My bum was numb from sitting there anyway.

'That's all right, Trish. Thanks for the *Star Trek*. I hadn't seen that one.'

'Come back later. I'm on till twelve.'

'Maybe. Depending on You Know Who.'

Trish shook her head. 'I know what I'd do with that fella.'

I nodded. 'The same thing I'd like to do with him.'

I zipped the jacket right up to my chin and stepped out into the wind. The town was busy with people jumping out of cars or going into the chipper. Mothers treating their kids. Like my mam used to treat me. Funny how almost everything reminded me of Mam. I'd be just walking along not feeling too bad, when a picture of her would pop into my head. Anything could cause it, from someone wearing a jumper like hers to a quick sniff of jasmine, her favourite perfume.

I put on my best hard face so no one would annoy me. You have to go around frowning in our estates, or the young lads will start hassling you on the way home. One chap tried it on me once, and I squirted ink all over his tracksuit top. He ran off home, squealing like a baby. These lads are very particular about their clothes. It's hard to be cool covered in blue squiggles. I always keep a magic marker in my pocket, just in case.

I took the long way around, even though the wind was blowing a hole in me. I could have cut across the green, past the swings. But I didn't. One, because that's where all the teenage couples hung out, and the boys would be only dying to make a show of some young one to impress their girlfriends. And two, because the quicker I got home, the quicker I'd have to look at Franco's greasy face.

The house was in an awful state. Even after four months. You'd think it'd take longer than that for a house to fall apart. But there were already green fingers creeping up the walls. The grass had crested the window ledges, and the gate hung limply from the hinges. Of course, when Mam was alive we wouldn't have tolerated any of this. The two of us would have been out with the sleeves rolled up doing whatever needed doing. That was back when number forty-seven had been a home. Now it was just a house.

Mam had never been very lucky with men. First my dad, who disappeared off to London at the first sign of responsibility on the horizon. And then Franco, probably the most useless, disgusting layabout ever to glue himself to a sofa with his own sweat. I could feel a shudder beginning at the base of my spine and working its way up. I couldn't help it. Every time I thought of that man …

I had developed a way to open the front door without a key. You put your shoulder in just the right spot and heaved. The frame was so warped that the lock just popped right out of its slot. Of course, Franco pounding on it every time he forgot his keys didn't help. It was handy, though, if you wanted to sneak in unnoticed.

I popped the door gently. As usual, the television was blaring from the sitting room. I didn't go in there any more, no matter what was on. That was Franco's room now, and he was welcome to it. No telly was a small price to pay for not having to look at his mug.

I had the stairs figured too. Every one of the steps was creaky, so you had to slot your feet into the gaps between the banisters and go up like a crab. Not too comfortable, but quiet.

I tiptoed across the landing and into my room. I was safe now. Franco might shout and roar, but he'd never drag his fat backside up the stairs after me. Too much effort.

I'm ashamed to admit it, but even my own room was a tip. Mam would've been disgusted. She wouldn't have stood for it. But Mam wasn't here. She was dead. Knocked down crossing a pedestrian walkway by a sleeping taxi driver on his third shift.

My schoolbag was lying in the corner where I'd tossed it that afternoon. There was homework in there waiting for me, like a beartrap in a hole. But I wouldn't do it. No point pretending. I was so far behind at this stage …

I decided to go out again. Maybe I'd have a night on the town. Hop on the supermarket bus and catch a late show in the cinema.

My money was well hidden. Tucked away with all my treasure. I'd figured that the one place Franco would never venture near was the bookshelf. So all my personal stuff was stashed inside a hollow binder for *The Lord of the Rings* box set.

I pulled the carton down, spilling my hoard on to the bed. The unmade bed. The unmade-for-about-two-months bed. If Mam had been alive, I wouldn't have been for much longer.

There was the shoelace bracelet given to me by Gerry Farrell, back in fourth class. And the essay certificate for that competition I'd won. 'The Whale: Our Gentle Friend'. And the petrified starfish I'd found on Curracloe beach. And Mam's engagement ring, the one she always said would be mine one day, and now it was. Years too soon.

I frowned. Where was the ring? Probably down in the corner of the box. Wedged in a cardboard flap. I groped around inside the container. Nothing. And my money. My two fifty. That was gone too. A sick feeling caught hold of my stomach, and clawed its way to the base of my throat. Franco!

I raced down the stairs, bouncing off the wall in my haste. Franco was, as usual, submerged in a cloud of smoke.

'Where is it?' I yelled, panic-stricken.

Franco never took his eyes off the screen.

'Where's what?' he asked, irritated that I'd corrupted his viewing environment.

'The ring!' I said, pointing to my finger where the ring should be. 'My mam's ring.'

Franco chewed on the filter of his cigarctte, mulling it over. 'Oh, the diamond ring. That ring?'

'Yes!' I nearly screamed. 'That ring.'

Franco stubbed out the butt in an overflowing ashtray.

'Well, you probably know that your mother wanted me to have that ring.'

I couldn't even deny it. My voice had deserted me.

'So … I sold it.'

They were simple words. But for some reason, I couldn't seem to understand them.

'You sold it?'

Franco nodded slowly. 'Yes, moron. I sold it. What did you think? You could hide it in your box forever?'

'But,' I stammered. 'But, but ...'

'But, but,' laughed Franco. 'What are you? One of those rappers. Look. I sold the ring. There you go. Boo hoo. Sob sob. Now get out of the way. I can't see my new television.'

My brain wouldn't focus. I remember trying to pin down the information that was flying at me, but it kept slipping away. One thing got through though. New television.

There it was, plonked in the middle of the sitting room, the light from its screen shining through the fog of cigarette smoke. Matt black and dangerous looking.

'Lovely, isn't she?' said Franco, a hitch in his voice. 'Dolby surround sound and teletext. Top of the range. Beautiful.'

I felt as though a steamroller had flattened my head, cartoon style. Mam's ring for this?

'That was all I had,' I said through gritted teeth, trying to hold back the tears. 'All I had left.'

'Yeah, yeah, whatever,' said Franco, waving me out of the way.

'And you sold it. For this.'

'At last. She gets the picture!' Franco laughed. It sounded like a frog in a barrel. 'That's funny really. Because I'm the one that got the picture. Do you get it?'

The television sat there. All flat screen and speakers. It was the only time I can remember hating a thing. So I attacked it. Or at least I tried to. Before I could do any real damage, Franco had me by the scruff of the neck and pinned against the wall. I couldn't believe he'd moved so fast.

'That's not allowed, Missy,' he said, his eyelids heavy and threatening.

'You had no right,' I mumbled, squirming to avoid his breath.

Franco laughed. 'No right? Let's talk about rights. You're under my charge. So you're the one with no rights. You're a juvenile, a known troublemaker. A nothing. Less than nothing. People are sorry for me. That poor man, they say. Trying to control that tearaway on his own. He's a saint. A martyr.'

I shut my eyes and mouth. Trying to block it all out.

'Your mother is dead, Missy. Dead! So stop pretending everything is the way it was. No more little miss happy princess. You will toe the line around here. You will pull your weight, and you will show *me* some respect. Or I'll be forced to sort you out, just like I did your mother! Her and her precious bottles of jasmine.'

Sorted out your mother? He'd hit Mam?

'You pig!' I sobbed. 'I'll get you. You and that telly!'

Franco froze. I'd threatened the TV.

'Some people just can't be told,' he said, and slapped me across the cheek. Hard. I slid down the wall, on to the floor. I felt as though I'd been branded.

'Never threaten the television again,' he shouted, leaning down to slap me again. 'Never, never, never!'

Each never was emphasized with another slap. I wanted to stand up and fight back. Sink my fist into his flabby gut and watch him gasping for air on the lino. But I couldn't. It was all too much for me. Pouring over my head like a suffocating wave. He was too big.

I was saved by the end of the advertisements. Distracted by a theme tune, Franco shuffled back to his throne. He sank into the chair, his thighs barely squeezing between the arms. I squatted on the floor like a battered spider, afraid to get up in case the movement attracted attention.

'Oh, and one more thing,' he said, patting his shirt pocket for matches. 'I've started official adoption proceedings. That means I get to stay here forever, and you get a brand new daddy. Wonderful news, eh?'

I didn't answer. It wasn't really a question. Pain and hatred were battling for attention in my head. The hatred won. You can't strike someone's mam and expect nothing to happen. Franco would have to pay for this. I didn't know how, just yet, but the atom of an idea was spinning in my brain. So he was fond of television, was he? Well, I'd just have to hit him where it hurt. Hit him hard.

CHAPTER 12: DOUBLE REVENGE

FRANCO was a man of few interests, and sharing a house with him meant that I knew them all. He could list them on the stubby fingers of one hand. Television, obviously, was the great love of his life. The cathode ray tube sang to him each day for a minimum of eight hours, overpowering the outside world with glamorous escapism. Food was high on the list. Convenience food by necessity, or else it would impinge on time allotted to TV. So, crisps, chocolate and delivery pizzas were the main staples. Drink was good. A semi-inebriated mind sinks all the more readily into the mire of satellite stations.

But this was the private Franco. One that the public never saw. Outside the warped door of his inherited house, Franco Kelly was a pillar of the community. A shaky pillar perhaps, but a pillar, nonetheless. Franco saw himself in the tragic hero mould. Loses the love of his life, but nobly sticks around to raise her brat of a kid.

To keep this legend going, Franco would strap on a suit and tie every Monday evening and stroll over to the Crescent Bar to chair a committee meeting of his beloved Newford Pigeon

Fanciers' Association. After the toilet and the fridge, the NPFA was probably the only thing that could tempt Franco out of his armchair. Not that he kept pigeons himself – that would have required effort. But you didn't have to own them to appreciate them, he reasoned. And hadn't he watched the club video until the tape snapped?

So, I plotted. The television and the NPFA. How could I combine the two in a suitably evil revenge plot? The answer came in fragments, like the pieces of a complicated jigsaw. There was preparation to be done. The first thing I needed was a video camera.

I borrowed the video camera from Belch, and set it up outside the back window. I worried a bit about that. Borrowing something from Belch. God only knew where he got a video camera – plus, he would want something in return. Probably a bit of help with one of his more dubious operations. I shrugged off the worry. Whatever it was, it'd be worth it.

I filmed my stepfather whenever the opportunity arose. I filmed him lounging around scratching himself, pouring beer over his peanuts. Staying in his vest and shorts for an entire weekend. Just excerpts, mind, when his attention was focused on the screen. Two whole days would have been far too harrowing for any viewer. I filmed him arguing with the TV, drooling in his sleep and basically humiliating himself in every way possible. But it wasn't enough. Not after what he'd done.

Step two. Incitement. I set the camera to record that Friday afternoon and ran around into the sitting room.

'Hey, Fatso,' I said. 'Give me a lend of a tenner.'

Franco stirred from a semi-doze. A ribbon of dried dribble cracked on his chin.

'Huh?'

'A tenner. You know, ten pounds. You understand that, don't you, chubby?'

Franco frowned. Was this brat ever going to learn? 'Watch your mouth, Missy. Don't make me get up out of this chair.'

I laughed. A sarcastic bark. 'Get up out of the chair? You? Don't make me laugh.'

Franco tried for a disbelieving chuckle, what came out was a strangled gasp. He was cracking. 'I'm warning you now, Missy!'

'You're warning me? You'd be better off warning a tortoise, that's about the only thing you could catch.'

Franco threw his belly forward, the shift in balance tumbling him from the chair. I made no attempt to escape. Why would I? This was the whole point. My stepfather punched me on the shoulder. A vicious dead-arm, with the middle knuckle pointed. I cried with pain. I wasn't acting.

'I used to play soccer you know,' pouted Franco, still wounded by the tortoise comment. 'That's where I got the name. Francooo, they used to shout every time I scored. And that was plenty of times, I can tell you.'

I wiped my eyes with the ragged sleeve of my school cardigan. Keep talking, fat boy. My plan was almost complete. Just one more incident to film.

It was Franco's custom to drink himself into a stupor on the weekend. He felt he deserved it after drinking himself into a stupor all week. By midnight on Sunday, World War Three under the armchair wouldn't wake him.

So I waited on the landing until his snores echoed up the stairs, then I sneaked down the stairway, crab-fashion, feet wedged between the banisters. I needn't have worried about stealth. Franco was dead to the world. He had changed into his drinking underwear, and was snoring up at least a force seven. I plucked a smouldering cigarette butt from between his fingers before it roused him, destroying all my plans.

The TV was still on. Some shoot 'em up movie. Franco's favourite, but not enough to keep him awake.

This was the tricky part. If I turned off the television now, Franco would wake up, for sure. I doubted he could sleep at all without the comforting blare from the idiot box. But I had a plan.

The old television was still in the corner, half-buried under burger cartons and fag boxes. I dragged it across the lino, plugging it into the double adapter. Now all I had to do was switch the aerial around and we were in business. There was a moment of hiss, then mono sound erupted from the old set. Franco never stirred.

I quickly unplugged the new set and wheeled it out the back door. Luckily the whole rig was on castors, so rolling it down to the shed was no problem. The camera was already set up. Now all I needed was the sledgehammer.

I remember squatting on the window ledge waiting for Franco to wake up. Giggles were spiralling in my throat, like caged hamsters. Hysteria I suppose, and fear.

Franco waking up was a slow process. It could go on for hours. First he might surface for a scratch, or maybe a quick shuffle to the bathroom, then he could sink into a stupor for another forty winks. I had turned off all the radiators to quicken up the performance.

At nine o' clock, his eyelids fluttered. A meaty hand patted the armchair for his cigarettes. Having located the box, he twisted one into the corner of his mouth and lit it with his lighter. All with his eyes closed.

He scraped his tongue along his top teeth and grimaced. The remains of last night's beer and fast food. A drink was called for.

Franco pulled his eyelids apart with the heels of his hands. Bloody lightning bolts shot through the whites. He was in a bad way. I knew how this was going. Soon he would descend into a murderous sulk, blaming the world for his self-inflicted hangover.

Then he paused. Something was wrong. Out of place. He took inventory. He was in his chair. Smoking his cigarette. Watching his ...

Franco leapt from the armchair. Oh my God! Shock and disbelief rippled down his face. What was happening? His TV! Gone!

I shot a close-up of his mug, praying for tears. I would not be disappointed.

Franco fell to his knees in front of the old television. There was a tape on the video. Play me, the note said.

With shaky fingers, Franco fumbled the cassette into the VHS. After a moment's hiss, two objects came into focus. One was me, the other was the TV.

'Nooo.'

The word leaked from between Franco's lips, like the last spurt of air from a balloon.

I couldn't hear my voice from outside the window, but I knew what I was saying.

'My dear stepdaddy. Because you paid for this TV with my ring, I think it legally belongs to me. So, *legally*, I can do whatever I like with it. I could sit down and watch "Glenroe". Or I could go to work on it with this!'

My television image pulled a tool from out of shot. It was a long-handled sledgehammer.

Franco stuffed eight fingers in his mouth. Pantomime terror. 'No, you little brat. No!'

Even if I did feel a moment of mercy then, the *me* on the television didn't. She laid into that TV with the gusto of a one-woman wrecking crew. She got really carried away, forgot all about the camera. It was a bit embarrassing really. Franco flinched with every blow.

'Stop. Please, stop. I'll give you anything.'

He was pawing the screen now, tears dribbling down his nose. It was pathetic. The man had barely shed a tear at my mother's funeral. And here he was, destroyed by the death of a television.

By the end, Franco was flat on the floor, hands over his ears to shut out the destruction. The television was little more than a box of glass and sparks. And I had every glorious moment on tape.

Needless to say, I kept well out of the way for the rest of the day. I can only imagine how Franco made it through until the meeting. Maybe that's what kept him going, the thought of a night out with the lads.

When I arrived at the NPFA AGM, he was every inch his public self, except for a slightly haunted cast about the eyes. The boys were set up in the lounge of the Crescent Bar, with the big screen all ready for the race video.

I counted to three and burst in the double doors. Franco's first impulse was to lunge, but he couldn't. Not with adoption papers in the works. You could buy another television. Houses were a bit harder to come by.

'What is it, Meg?' he said through clenched teeth. 'You should be in bed. It's a school night.'

'I have your tape, Uncle Franco,' I said, staring him straight in the eye. 'You forgot it.'

Franco blinked. 'What tape?'

'The Dover Pigeon Grand Prix. For after the meeting.'

Franco checked his bag. The tape wasn't there. How could it be, seeing as I had buried it at the bottom of our bin. He took the cassette tentatively, as though it might explode.

'Thanks, girl,' he muttered. 'Off home with you now.'

I pulled a sulky face. 'Aw. Can't I watch? Pigeon racing is so cool.' Flattery will get you anywhere.

'Ah, let the girl stay, Franco. Be a treat for her.'

'One night out, Chairman. It won't kill her.'

What could my stepfather do? He couldn't be ungracious in front of his peers, yet he suspected a trap.

'OK, Meg,' he said at last. 'But we'll have a little talk about this later.'

A perfectly innocent statement. To all ears but mine. I knew what Franco meant by 'a little talk'.

So they put on the tape. I watched, spellbound, as it slid into the recorder, whirring gently into its groove. Surely my plan could not work. Surely someone would stop me. But no. It not only worked, it was perfect.

For a few seconds there was mild puzzlement, as even Franco didn't recognize himself. Then the laughter started. It began in the back of the lounge, well away from the committee table. But it spread like the sunrise, creeping up the room, touching everyone present.

Except two. Franco wasn't laughing. And neither was I.

It was comical, in a pathetic sort of way. This bloated bighead exposed as the layabout I knew him to be. There were plenty of pigeon fanciers delighted to have the chance for a giggle at their pompous chairman.

The laughing stopped pretty sharpish during the boxing scene. Nobody thought hitting children was funny. But I like to leave them laughing, so I kept the TV destruction scene till last. Rolling in the aisles, they were.

I remember a cold satisfaction creeping across my heart. I had destroyed Franco twice. Once on tape and once in person. One for Mam and one for me. He stormed from the meeting, tears of shame coursing down his cheeks. He would resign from the NPFA the following day. By letter.

Naturally, Franco's plans for adoption were up the spout. He could do what he liked now, but he'd never be my father.

Belch came visiting the next day. Calling in his favour. He wanted me to stand guard over a granny-flat burglary. A break-in. My first. I remember thinking that it shouldn't be too dangerous.

Lowrie had sobered up considerably.

'That ...' he couldn't finish the sentence. Not in front of a minor.

Meg laughed bitterly. 'You might as well say it. I can see your thoughts anyway.'

But Lowrie couldn't. His own decency wouldn't let him.

'That ... pig,' he said instead.

'Tell me about it.'

'Still, that was a devious plot you hatched against him.'

Meg's eyes were like stone. 'He shouldn't have hit my mam.'

Lowrie nodded. How could you argue with that?

'So, can I have it?' asked Meg.

'Hmm?'

'The spare wish. Can I have it?'

Lowrie scratched his chin. The bristles were beginning to poke through again after his facial.

'Yes,' he said finally. 'You can have it. And, what's more, I'll add whatever strength I have to the punch.'

Meg grinned, and there was nothing angelic about it.

Belch stared at his hairy hands.

'I'm fading away,' he whined. And that's not just a descriptive verb. He actually was whining.

Elph ran a systems check.

'Your ecto cranium was perforated in the explosion.'

'Arf?'

'There's a hole in your head,' sighed the hologram. 'We're leaking life force. There's only minutes left before we are pulled back to headquarters.'

'What happens then?'

Elph consulted a memory file. 'You will go to work as a spit turner on the dung plain. I will be ... I don't know what I will be. There's no precedent. But I would surmise that it will be something bad.'

'Isn't there anything we can do? There must be some way of stealing some of this life force stuff?'

The hologram buzzed through his hard-drive infernopedia. 'Negative. There is no permitted method.'

Belch's wet nose quivered. 'Permitted? No *permitted* method.'

Elph looked uncomfortable, which isn't easy for a hologram. It involves a lot of pixel rearrangement.

'There is one way. Totally forbidden. The possible ramifications are enormous.'

'Arf?'

'It could cause a lot of trouble here on Earth.'

Belch shrugged. 'So what are they going to do? Plug you out and make me a spit turner?'

'I see your point.'

Belch couldn't believe it. At last he'd made a point! 'So, what is this forbidden way?'

Elph hovered across the room to Franco, who was blissfully unaware of all this supernatural intrusion.

'To put it in moron's terms, we need an extra battery. I've run a scan on this lifeform and he has twenty-six years of juice left in him.'

Belch licked his lips. 'Twenty-six years?'

'Of course, running two entities and a parallel port hologram would bring that down to … twenty-six hours. But it's better than nothing. All you need to do is possess him, and siphon off some of his life force. You'll find it just above the eyeballs. Bright orange. You can't miss it.'

'Right. So let's do it,' Belch paused. 'One more thing. I want him to see me.'

'Whatever for?'

Belch raised his furry paw/hands. 'Because what's the point of being like this if I can't scare anybody?'

Elph nodded. He understood perfectly. He was, after all, a demon hologram.

Franco was in a foul mood. There was a gap in the curtains and the light was reflecting off the TV screen. It was affecting his viewing pleasure. Fixing it would mean getting up out of the chair. Franco decided to wait it out. There was only news on at the moment anyway.

Suddenly he had a vision. There was a werewolf-type creature standing before him. It just materialized out of thin

air. Franco wasn't worried. He'd been expecting hallucinations for some time. He'd seen it on the science channel
where people who deprived themselves of reality often saw
phantom images. Franco regarded this experience as an
extra channel.

'Hello, doggy,' he said reaching out to tickle it under the
chin.

The creature growled and batted away his hand. For a
moment they connected, and Franco saw everything. He saw
and understood everything.

'Oh no,' he breathed, the wastefulness of his life stretching
out behind him.

'Oh yes,' grinned Belch. 'It's me. I'm back and I've come
to eat your soul.'

Franco began to scream. He continued to scream as the
creature invaded his mind and began feeding on his essence.
He continued to scream even as he was banished to a musty
corner of his own brain, and no one could hear him anymore.

Meg's fingers were fading too.

'Not much time left,' she observed, wiggling the ghostly
digits. 'How do I look?'

'A ghost of your former self.'

'That's not funny.'

'Sorry. I'm a bit nervous. We are going to assault someone
in broad daylight, after all.'

Meg curled her transparent hand into a fist. She just prayed
she'd have enough strength left to knock her stepfather's
block off.

'No chat now,' she warned. 'I just want to whack him and
get out of here.'

'No argument from me.'

They were outside the gate now. Or, rather, where the gate used to be. All that was left was a single drooping hinge. The rest lay partially buried in the grass. The walls had deteriorated too. Wild ivy shoots were scrabbling across the stucco and the paint had long since faded to reveal a dirty concrete colour beneath.

Lowrie followed the driveway to the door. At least he presumed it was the driveway. It was difficult to pinpoint beneath the treacherous carpet of weeds.

'OK. Here we are.'

Meg took a deep breath and climbed into Lowrie's head. She could feel the strain tugging at her essence. There were only a couple of possessions left in her, then it was back up the tunnel.

Maybe coming here was stupid. A waste of energy. They could be halfway through Lowrie's final wish now, instead of risking both their immortal souls on a silly stunt. Then Meg thought of someone laying a finger on her mam, and her resolve returned.

'OK,' she beamed at Lowrie's half of the brain. 'Knock knock. Wallop! Bye-bye. Couldn't be easier.'

Meg raised her now arthritic finger to the buzzer. But it was gone. There was a bell-shaped gap in the paintwork, but no bell. Another repair neglected by Franco. She rapped on the frosted glass. It stung her knuckles. Lowrie's feelings were beginning to surmount her own.

'Someone's coming,' said Lowrie, taking control of his mouth for a second.

Meg blinked a bead of sweat from Lowrie's eye. Her own nervousness was sending the old man's sweat glands into overdrive. She pulled back a fist. As soon as the door cracked open. Pow! He'd never know what hit him. It might cost a few centuries in purgatory, but it'd be worth it.

A shadowy figure was loping up the hallway, diffracted by the bubble glass. It was Franco, all right. No doubt about it, even with the pane's distortion. Come on, fat boy. Open your mouth and say cheese.

The door swung open. A face appeared. Meg swung.

And in the time between swing and impact, time seemed to decelerate. Just long enough for the head to speak.

'Hello, Finn. I've been expecting you.'

Odd, thought Meg. Franco never called her Finn. Only Missy. Also, how did he know it was her? And why was he slobbering? Then the punch landed and Franco collapsed like a sack of pig dung.

'Nice one,' enthused Lowrie. 'Now, off we go.'

But Meg couldn't go. There was something wrong here. She strode into the hallway of number forty-seven, slamming the door behind her.

Franco was writhing on the floor. Whining and slobbering.

Slobbering? Whining? Suddenly it was all too clear. She squinted at the fallen figure, using her own eyes this time. And there he was, floating inside her stepfather, his bestial face twisted by hate.

'Belch!' she exclaimed.

Her enemy did not answer, except to snarl and spit. Clearly his human half took a back seat under pressure.

'What are you doing here?'

Belch squinted through a haze of pain.

'I've come for you, Finn. The Master wants your soul.'

A small figure in white popped out of Franco's head and began to hover over the fallen figure.

'There is no need to provide the target with information. Just get up and do your job.'

Meg nodded at the white-suited hologram. 'What the hell is that?'

'Do us both a favour, Finn, and squash it like a bug!'

Elph managed to look injured. 'After all I've done for you. If it wasn't for me, you'd be turning spits long ago. Now, finish siphoning and get these two.'

Belch opened his mouth and began to suck. Glittering orange strings erupted behind Franco's eyes and flowed down the demon's throat. With every gulp he grew stronger, more *there*.

'Uh oh,' said Meg and Lowrie together.

Franco was changing. As his life force was devoured, his body paid the price. Deep lines etched themselves across his forehead. His eyes lost their shine and sank into his face. The flesh on his neck drooped and sagged. It was still Franco, but twenty years older.

'This is not good,' muttered Meg. 'I have to do something.'

Elph whirred across the room, hovering not five centimetres from Lowrie's nose. He chuckled, purely for effect, since holograms have no sense of humour.

'What you will do, Meg Finn, is fail. Then you will return below with us. My creator will be exalted above that buffoon Beelzebub, and your old man will die unfulfilled. That is what you will do.'

Meg snarled. For once Belch was right. She should squash this annoying thing like a bug. She grabbed a vase from the hall dresser and hurled it at the flickering hologram. Of course it passed straight through, impacting on the crown of Franco's head. The result was spectacular. What you'd expect when a vase hit a head was: ow! Possibly a small gash. Concussion at the very most. Certainly no more than that. What Meg got was a sudden unearthly light display, as the vase's contents distributed themselves across Franco's head. The dust fizzled and crackled, sealing itself like concrete to her stepfather's face. Franco screamed, and Belch howled. It was a grating combination. Glasses popped in the kitchen, windows shattered. Even Franco's precious TV tube succumbed to the sonic waves, imploding into a thousand pieces.

Franco writhed on the hall floor, scraping at his own face, but it was no use. The dust had adhered itself in a viscous sheet over his entire upper body.

Elph watched dispassionately from a height. 'Hmm. Interesting. Violent allergic reaction of the painful kind.' The hologram ran a match on the word *allergy*. 'Only one hit. Allergy. A malignant spirit may display signs of discomfort when it comes in contact with a blessed substance.'

Meg retrieved a section of the vase. There was a brass nameplate near the base. Now she remembered. It was her mother's urn. From the crematorium.

'Mam,' she whispered, a tear slipping between her lashes.

Elph nodded. 'Blessed ashes. I would concur with that analysis.'

Meg aimed a kick at Franco's leg.

'You wouldn't even put the urn in the glass case.'

'He does regret that now,' noted Elph.

Franco couldn't answer. He could only share the pain inside his head. He wriggled and jerked for several moments before the agony knocked both him and his demonic lodger unconscious.

Meg gave him another belt on the leg. 'Serves you right. You two belong together.' She slipped the shard into Lowrie's pocket. 'Thanks, Mam. You saved me again.'

Lowrie took control of his mouth. 'Let's go, Meg. Before we all run out of time. That monster won't stay down forever.'

Meg blinked away her tears. It was true. She could feel herself fading away by the second, and they had a long way to go for the last wish.

'OK, Meggy,' she told herself in her mother's tones. 'Get a grip. You'll have all eternity to mope about. Finish the list! Only one more to go!'

She pointed a stiff finger at Elph. 'And as for you. If I ever see you again, you'll be pulling that lens out of your ear.'

'Me?' said Elph innocently. 'How would you ever see me again? I'm stuck with these two.'

But as soon as Lowrie's back was turned, Elph blinked, flashing a blue laser down the old man's frame. It was totally painless and only lasted a millisecond. But it was the one thing that could save the moron, and therefore the hologram itself, from the wrath of the Devil.

After the target and the human had disappeared down the hall, Elph rewound the last few minutes' video in his head. The girl had made a remark. Something that could be important. He scanned the VT for the appropriate moment. Finish the list, the girl had said. Hmm. What list would that be? And could it be the key to her damnation?

Elph stopped himself. There was no point to supposition. He would put himself on energy save mode until the idiot host awoke. He blinked once and disappeared. And there was no sign of life in number forty-seven except for the blinking red light of a standby button.

CHAPTER 13: FROM A GREAT HEIGHT

LOWRIE had gone mental, and rented a car.

'Might as well,' he reasoned. 'I've a feeling we don't have a lot of time left.'

Meg had the same feeling. She felt about as substantial as the morning dew, and her strength was fading with every mile. The Belch thing had shaken her. Who was the Master? And why did he want her soul? Meg had a dreadful suspicion that she knew the answer to both these questions. She could feel the tunnel now too. Its pulse pumped through her body, pulling her. Reminding her.

Not just a car either, to get back to their transport. A Peugeot coupé. All wheels and exhaust. Generally Meg would have been hopping around with excitement, pressing every button on the dash, but not today. Today neither passenger nor driver had the energy for anything besides essentials.

'Your last wish. Spit over the Cliffs of Moher,' said Meg, a slight chatter in her voice. 'What does *that* mean?'

'Exactly that,' responded Lowrie, shifting the stubby gearstick up into fifth. 'Like in the song.'

'What song?'

Lowrie rolled his eyes. 'Youngsters. What song? Didn't you learn anything in those schools?'

'Just sums and reading. Nothing useful like spitting songs.'

Lowrie tapped out a rhythm on the racing steering wheel, and after a few bars he began singing in a grating Dubliners' kind of a voice.

'To have lived a life to the full,
A man must have broken every rule,
Slept in a ditch,
Married a witch.
To have lived his life to the full.

To appreciate life as much as you can,
You must kiss the sweetheart of another man,
Spit right over,
The Cliffs of Moher,
To appreciate life as much as you can …'

'I could go on. There are forty-seven verses.'

'No, that's all right,' said Meg hurriedly. 'I get the picture. So we're doing this all because of some old song?'

'My father used to sing it to me. Every night at bedtime. It was our own lullaby. Mother didn't approve. The "marry a witch" line annoyed her slightly.'

'I wonder why.'

Lowrie chuckled. 'Not very politically correct, I know. But I have done that and all the rest in my time. Slept in a ditch and so on. But I didn't actually …'

'Spit over the Cliffs of Moher,' completed Meg. 'So what do you need me for?'

Lowrie rubbed his chest. 'The climb. I don't think I can make it.'

'More climbing,' grumbled Meg. 'That's just great. I hope heaven is worth it. I suppose I should be grateful your dad didn't know any songs about toilet cleaning, or we'd be doing that too.'

Time was of the essence. Elph knew that, so he decided to give Belch a little help regaining consciousness. A 'little help' consisted of a level-three positron shock to the hairy rump.

Belch spasmed. Franco spasmed too, seeing as Belch was still occupying his body. The dog-boy sat up sluggishly.

'Arf?' he enquired dopily.

'The target struck your host with some blessed ashes. As a malignant spirit, you are highly allergic.'

'Sore,' moaned Belch, apparently abandoning complete sentences in favour of single words. 'Itchy.'

'Quite,' said Elph, without the smallest trace of sympathy. 'Now get yourself out of that body. We have work to do, and very little time in which to do it.'

'Woof!' agreed Belch. He took a deep breath and attempted to slide out of Franco's body. It was no use. Something was holding him in. He tried again, face twisted with effort, but the spirit could not detach himself. 'Stuck.'

Elph chewed an electronic lip.

'I was afraid of this.'

'Arf?'

'The positively charged ashes are repelling your negative demonic force from all sides, creating an impermeable ectoshell.'

'Arf?'

'You're trapped. Stuck in that body. Which is a pity since you've already drained most of the life force.'

Belch studied his new fingers. They were yellow and wrinkled. Franco had aged thirty years. And he hadn't looked that good at thirty-five.

'Stuck? Noooo!'

'*Noooo!*' mimicked Elph dramatically. 'Grow up, idiot. Our mission is still the same. Find the old man. Stop the girl. Nothing has changed. As soon as we are successful, you'll be your own two selves again.'

Belch picked a scrap of stale food from Franco's dressing gown and stuffed it into his mouth.

'Food,' he growled. 'Good.'

Elph rolled his eyes, another affectation. 'For Satan's sake! We have more important things to think about than you feeding your face. Our strength grows weaker every minute.'

Belch concentrated for a moment, stringing a sentence together. 'Finn is gone. We don't know where. We're too late.'

'That's where you're wrong, oh moronic one. I, unlike you, take precautions against such eventualities.'

Belch's head was beginning to hurt. He didn't know whether it was the hole in his skull, or the hologram's continuous insults. 'What ... precautions?'

Elph felt the need to deliver a lecture. 'The ecto link and help program comes complete with a wraparound laser scanner. The very latest, not even available in Japan, something about corrosive side-effects on skin tissue. So before the old man left, I scanned his frame. I can do a three-sixty reconstruction. Maybe we can learn something.'

'Woof,' said Belch.

The hologram blinked and a computer reconstruction of Lowrie McCall appeared in the air before them. It consisted entirely of a matrix of green lines.

'Not very lifelike,' mumbled Belch.

'I'm running the program on a minimum memory, powered by the very limited electric pulses of your brain,' retorted the hologram. 'I could improve the rendering but it might knock you unconscious. Now, Finn mentioned something about a list ...'

Elph rotated the laser model. 'I'll just activate the x-ray tool. This uses over a hundred megabytes, so you may feel a tiny pinch ...'

As usual, Elph had understated the pain factor. Belch fell writhing on the floor, his eyeballs jittering like dice in a cup. In mid-air, Lowrie's clothes became transparent. The contents of his pockets became instantly visible.

'Breast pocket. Enhance,' ordered Elph.

Lowrie's pocket grew to A4 size.

'What have we here?'

Belch didn't answer, too busy slapping out the fire in Franco's hair.

'Grid reference X1,Y3, Z4. Enhance and unfold.'

Everything disappeared except the note. It grew to the size of the wall, and unfolded along the creases.

'Incredible. Based on residual ink traces on the reverse side, the program can accurately reconstruct the writing.'

Fascinating, Belch might have said, if he'd been in the mood for sarcasm, and not blubbering with fiery agony.

'This would be the list. A Wish List, if I'm not mistaken. Very common among the terminally pathetic. I'm surprised you don't have one, considering the mess you made of your life.'

Belch's brain felt like a bruised orange. Spit-turning couldn't be worse than this.

Elph ran a hinged finger down the list. *Only one more to go*, Finn had said. The last wish was ...

'Spit over the Cliffs of Moher? Why? Surely nobody would actually want to spit over a cliff.'

Elph shut down the program. 'Then again, these Irish are a strange race. Spitting over cliffs is exactly the kind of activity they would enjoy.'

He turned to the quivering mass on the floor. 'The Cliffs of Moher. Where are they?'

Belch searched his last few brain cells — the remaining couple not fried by Elph's meddling. The Cliffs of Moher. They did sound familiar.

'School tour,' he gasped.

'Say no more,' sighed Elph. 'I will search your memory files. Pictures say more than your vocabulary ever could.'

The hologram was silent for a moment, mentally thumbing through old experiences. Belch was glad of the respite.

'I have located these cliffs,' said Elph, all too quickly. 'The island's west coast. In the area known as County Clare.'

'That's right,' said Belch. 'County Clare.'

'Of course it's right, imbecile. Your own memory told me. To disagree would mean arguing with yourself.'

Belch risked a warning growl. Once they were in hell, he would make sure this nasty little gremlin got what was coming to him. 'So what do we do now? Just fly off across the country?'

'No, cretin. You are trapped in a human body. We are restricted to terrestrial transport. Does this human have a car?'

Belch chuckled. 'Franco? You must be joking. Sure, he never goes anywhere further than the bathroom.'

Elph blinked. 'Then we must acquire transport.'

'Acquire?'

'Yes. Acquire.'

Rissole O'Mahoney was taking a spin around the estates on his Honda Goldwing. He wasn't going anywhere special, just giving the local lads a chance to drool at his jet black speed-machine. You could get away with that when you were the hardest man in the area. Nobody else would draw attention to the fact that they had a five-thousand-pound bike parked in the driveway. But who'd be crazy enough to touch Rissole's bike? No one who wanted to live to ride it, that was for sure. Even the birds were too scared of Rissole to poop on his bike.

There was a drizzle coming down. The beginning of a storm, the chap on the telly said. So Rissole decided to head on home and put the bike under a tarp. You couldn't be too careful. Not with all the acid rain around these days.

He twisted the throttle a bit more than was necessary, pulling the Honda in a tight curve. Then he saw Franco Kelly standing in the road before him. In a dressing gown and slippers! The damp had pasted his hair to his skull, and his vest had moulded itself to a protruding belly.

Rissole put the bike in neutral and coasted over to his neighbour.

'Howye, Franco ...' he began, then stopped. It was Franco. He was sure of it. But the man seemed to have aged thirty years overnight.

'You should give up that drink, and start taking a bit of exercise,' advised Rissole. 'You look like a shadow of your da.'

Rissole chuckled. A shadow of your Da. Witty and hard. What a combination.

Franco wasn't laughing.

'Get off the bike,' he said, rain and drool spilling in strings off his chin.

The drooling should have given Rissole a hint that something wasn't right here. But he was too busy being the tough guy.

'What did you say, Franco?'

The thing that looked like his next-door neighbour growled – yes, actually growled, at him.

'My name is not Franco, and I said get off the bike.'

Rissole sighed. He'd given your man a chance. Been nice and everything. What choice did he have except to dish out a few punches.

'Now, listen to me, Kelly …' he began, flicking down the stand with his boot. That was all he said, except for 'Aaaeerrgghhh.' Which is not really a word. But the reason that he screamed aaaeerrggghhh, was that Franco had bitten him savagely on the wrist. He just took the skin between his teeth and worried it until a large section tore off.

Rissole collapsed on the tarmac, gibbering. He'd been in a hundred bar-room brawls, but this! This was different. Animal.

'Calm down, Franco,' he stuttered, holding his injured forearm close to his chest. 'What's the problem?'

Belch squatted down on his hunkers. He could smell fear. It was nice.

'No problem,' he grunted. 'I need your bike.'

Rissole opened his mouth to object. Then he noticed a trickle of blood rolling from the corner of Franco's lips.

'OK. Take it. Take it.'

Belch nodded. Pleased with the consternation he was causing. 'There's something else,' he said, spitting out a fold of skin.

'Yes. What? Anything. Anything.'

Belch rubbed the sleeve of Rissole's biker jacket.

'Your clothes. Take them off.'

Flit, the tunnel mite, was up for probation. He was feeling very insecure at the moment, sitting in front of the great Saint Peter wearing nothing but a cheesy grin and a sooty old loin cloth.

'Sooo,' mused Peter, calling up Flit's file on his monitor. 'Tell me you've changed.'

Flit's head bobbed enthusiastically. 'Flit changed. Much changed. Different I entirely.'

Peter sighed. 'I'm not feeling it, Flit. Make me believe it.' There were those who said, very quietly, that Saint Peter spent far too much time with his monitor tuned to terrestrial talk shows, and was beginning to fancy himself as an amateur sociologist.

'Flit worky hard. All the time. Worky worky worky. Never stop to suck stones like Crank and other mites.'

'I see. And are you sorry, Flit? Do you regret your crimes?'

Flit squeezed an aquamarine tear from the corner of his eye. 'Oh yes. Sorry in every bone. Cry all time. When not worky worky worky. Poor poor people. How could Flit take their money? Bad Flit, bad!'

Flit slapped himself on the wrist to demonstrate his remorse. Not too hard.

'Hmmm,' said Peter doubtfully. 'I suppose you have filled your baskets. But before I grant you access to everlasting bliss, there's just one question.' He leaned forward until they were nose to nose. 'And remember, you cannot lie. Instant disqualification.'

The tunnel mite's Adam's apple bobbed in his throat. 'Flit remember. No lie.'

Peter settled back. 'Good. If you arrived at the gates, and they were unguarded, would you sneak in?'

Flit wrung his bony fingers. He couldn't lie. Peter would smell it in every pore of his blue body.

'Yes,' he cried in anguish. 'Flit would. Sneak right in. Tip toe tip. True true true. Bad but true.'

Peter's face was stony. A poker face.

'Hmm,' he said reaching for the limbo button. 'I don't know. It's just so close. OK, so you told the truth, but the truth was bad. If only you'd ever done something to help somebody. Something selfless.'

Flit racked his addled brain. How could he have helped somebody since his last interview? He'd been in the tunnel. And nobody ever stopped long enough to be helped. Flit sucked in a sharp breath. Nobody except …

'Sainty gateman,' he blurted. 'No press button, pull lever. Flit help. Flit help girl.'

Something in the tunnel mite's tone stayed Peter's hand.

'Flit help what girl?'

The coupé sped west, crunching the cross-country miles. Outside the streamlined bodywork, nature mixed some turmoil in the skies. Stirring up rain in the bellies of clouds, and throwing lightning bolts across their underbellies. Real melodramatic stuff.

The car's occupants weren't saying much. The end was coming, one way or the other. They both knew it. It was just a question of which one of them would go through the tunnel first. And when that person came to the fork, would it be up, or down …?

Lowrie's heart was on its last few beats. He could feel the organ shutting down, every spurt of blood a struggle. The pills were no good any more. Every breath could be his last. It felt worse now, somehow. Now that he had rediscovered himself. There was more to lose.

Meg felt as if she should be somewhere else. Somewhere blue. The tunnel's heartbeat was pumping through her veins. She had only hours left. Maybe minutes.

They had to drive clear across Ireland to reach the Cliffs of Moher. But, as any American will tell you, they spit further'n that. In spite of geography, the journey seemed a long one. Especially with the regrets of two souls swirling around the cab like depressed fog.

Finally, three hours and countless picture-postcard towns later, they made it. The Cliffs of Moher. Closed. Or so the sign said.

'Closed?' scoffed Meg. 'How can you close a cliff?'

Lowrie pointed to the chain across the carpark entrance. 'Just like that.'

It made sense really. The drizzle had thickened to full-blown rain, and a treacherous wind was rocking the car on its axles. Blustery clouds were threatening lightning. Positive and negative charges gearing up for the big grounding.

'Hmm,' mumbled Lowrie.

A sudden gust of wind could catch hold of a person on those cliffs and whip them into the abyss. Not to mention the fact that you'd be a virtual lightning rod standing up on that plateau.

Meg read the emotions swirling above his head. 'You're right,' she said. 'We should give up.'

Lowrie opened the door with his shoulder. 'There'll be no more giving up. Not today.'

And he was gone into the storm.

Saint Peter was trying not to think about it. Concentrate on something else, he told himself. Your desk, or those exotic birds, or the splendour of the tunnel. Or one of the other things he'd been staring at for the last two thousand years.

It was forbidden, strictly forbidden, to get involved. Oh, but it would be sweet to snatch a soul from under Bub's fangs. Sure, his demonic counterpart made noises about being replaced, but he would weather the storm. And if the girl deserved an interview at the Pearlies, then that's what she should receive.

But there was no point even thinking about it. Interference was out of the question. Every single time spirits got involved, things went horribly astray. Angels and mortals. Oil and water. They don't mix.

It'd be different if Beelzebub had sent in a Soul Man. Then he'd just be evening up the odds. Everyone deserved an equal shot at redemption. Even the Man Himself agreed with that. Every sparrow on the branch and so on.

So, Peter persuaded himself, Beelzebub being a demon had most likely sent someone back to retrieve the Irish girl's soul. In that case, it was his angelic duty to send someone for a peek down the tunnel. Just to see what was going on.

A flimsy argument, true. But Peter was a tad bored after two thousand years on that marble chair.

*

The Cliffs of Moher were an awesome sight, even for someone who'd travelled the length of the tunnel. They loomed above the ocean. Vast sheets of grey rock, arranged in a ragged horseshoe over the roughest patch of coastline in Ireland. It was easy to imagine that the cliffs were the bite pattern of some gigantic prehistoric sea monster.

The wind tugged at Lowrie's blazer and prodded at the bend in his weak knee. Rain found its way into his eyes, obscuring his vision and blurring the cliff's edge.

'Come on!' he shouted above the crash of the waves. 'Before I lose my nerve!'

Ahead, in the distance, a round tower sat perched on the cliff apex. The perfect vantage point.

'It has to be up there, I suppose?'

Lowrie nodded. 'Verse twenty-two. The very top.'

Meg scowled, slipping into Lowrie's head for the last time. It was hard. Very hard. Like climbing through a wall of slick mud.

'Are you there?' asked Lowrie.

An ominous question. He should be able to feel her immediately. Her youth and vitality. But now his strength was almost as great as her own.

Meg flexed the old man's fingers. 'Yes. I'm here. Just about. Don't go away though. It'll take two of us to climb this hill.'

They turned into the wind and put Lowrie's weight into it. Of course Lowrie, being an old bachelor, weighed about as much as a sack of feathers and would be more use as a hang-glider than a paperweight. You could almost hear the wind sniggering.

But they kept going, squatting low to the ground at first, then on hands and knees. Meg opened Lowrie's mouth to complain, but a gust of wind saw its chance and sent a swirling tendril of compressed air down his gullet, with a few leaves mixed in for good measure. Meg kept the mouth shut after that.

Franco's body was just a husk at this stage. Belch was sucking his juices as fast as his neuro cortex could absorb them.

'Good stuff,' he dribbled, orange gunge slathered over his ecto chops.

'You might consider pacing yourself,' commented Elph, effortlessly floating abreast of the Goldwing. 'Save some essence for the assault. There will be some mayhem to be created when we reach the target zone.'

'Maybe I should turn *you* off. Save some energy.'

Elph laughed. 'Turn me off! And leave you in charge of the mission! That would be akin to asking a baboon to program the video recorder.'

That was probably an insult, but Belch didn't waste time thinking about it. He didn't have the energy. Franco's fluids were running out fast. They were coming in spurts now rather than a steady flow. He felt like a kid chasing the last drop of cola with a straw. This was going to be a real nailbiter of a finish.

Meg looked up to check their progress. 'I don't believe it,' she groaned. 'We're further away!'

She knew it wasn't true, that it only felt like that, but she couldn't help being disheartened all the same. The rain was pummelling them now. Drops the size of bullseyes lashed on to Lowrie's bare scalp. His heart was hopping like a steamhammer in a hole and his limbs were weakening from irregular blood supply. Meg poured her strength into him. Every ounce she had. But it wasn't going to be enough. It was just too far.

'Come on, Lowrie!' she broadcast. 'Do it here! For God's sake. This isn't important. Not like Sissy. Just spit and go home.'

Deep inside his own mind Lowrie considered it. He was killing what was left of this girl, and for what? The memory of a lullaby? She was right. He was a stupid old man.

'OK,' he thought. 'Let's do it here.'

'At last. You've switched on your brain.'

She turned Lowrie's back to the wind and leaned against the safety fence. There were at least two metres on the other side to the cliff's edge. She'd have to go over.

'Remember,' Lowrie advised her, 'you might be able to fly. But I can't. Not yet.'

'Don't tempt me,' grunted Meg, straddling the fence. Keeping one hand on the top rail, she edged towards the drop. The boom of the waves travelled up the sheer wall to pour over them like a physical force. It was awesome, terrifying.

Meg sniffed mightily, summoning a big ball of spit.

''Ere wee oo,' she mumbled around the liquid, and let fly. Right on to Lowrie's two-hundred-pound brogues. Why didn't anything ever go right the first time?

'Well?' growled Belch. 'You see anything?'

'Quiet!' snapped the hologram. 'I'm scanning.'

The bike was idling beside the visitors' centre. Elph was having problem with the electricity build-up in the atmosphere. It was scrambling his radar. He switched to ultra violet.

'Up there!' he buzzed triumphantly. 'On the ridge.'

Belch's canine night vision picked them out immediately. Right out on the cliff edge.

'Too easy,' he grinned, gunning the bike straight through the safety chain.

Funny how you never can spit when you need to. Funny — unless you're hanging over the edge of a two-hundred-metre drop into bone-crushing breakers.

Meg gargled energetically, conjuring images of all those foul cigars Lowrie smoked. Surely they had deposited some good-consistency phlegm in the lining of his throat. Nothing. Dry as a desert bone. Every spare drop of liquid had gone through the pores for perspiration.

'I don't believe it!' she shouted into the gale.

In sympathy, nature threw a lightning bolt across their bows. It impacted in the clay, showering them with sods.

Meg ducked low to avoid the missiles, and beneath the crook of Lowrie's arm she caught sight of Franco. On a motorbike. Coming straight for her.

'Oh …' she began, and that was as far as she got. Which was just as well.

Belch had just turned sixteen when he blew himself up. Sixteen. Old enough for a motorbike licence. That had been his plan. Break into McCall's. Sell his stuff. Buy a bike. Cruise around the estates with Rissole. Cool.

Luckily for Meg, this plan had never materialized. Because if Belch had been an expert instead of a novice, he would never have tried to ramp the fence. He would have simply bulled straight through it. That being the case, everyone involved in this little supernatural drama would have been dragged screaming, or howling, over the cliffs.

However, seeing as this was only Belch's third time on a motorcycle, he thought it would be extremely impressive to pull the front wheel over the top of the fence and drag the rest of the bike after it. No way, José, as Evel Knievel might have quipped. You need a ramp for that sort of stunt. And Belch didn't have a ramp.

The bike entangled itself in the chain link, roaring like a trapped animal. Franco's abused body sailed over the top rail straight on to Lowrie's chest. The foursome skidded across the rain-slickened muck to the very brink of the cliff.

Meg and Belch only had eyes for each other. Not in the usual romantic sense.

'It's all over, Finn!' growled the canine hybrid. 'You're coming with me!'

Meg grimaced as Franco's fingers grabbed at Lowrie's face. With that face so close to hers, it was like being alive again.

'Get off!' she sobbed. 'Leave me alone!'

'Get off!' mimicked Belch. 'Leave me alone! You're a sad case.'

Lowrie's heart was speeding up like cards on bicycle spokes. His breath was fading. Spots danced before his eyes. There was pain now too. Pain that felt red.

'Go!' Meg panted.

Lowrie couldn't even answer.

'Go now. I'll hold him!'

'What?'

'Go and spit over the edge. Then we win!'

Inside his own skull, Lowrie nodded. Meg was right. The only way to dispatch these two was to complete the list.

Meg peeled herself away, taking a tight grip on Franco's throat. There were no more tears now. Just determination. Not for herself, for her partner.

'*We* can still split up,' she grunted, putting every atom of strength into choking her nemesis. 'You can't, can you? That means Lowrie just has to crawl to the edge and we've won. And you know what that means, don't you?'

Belch's eyes widened. This couldn't be happening. He searched feverishly for a drop of juice in Franco's skull. But there was nothing. Sucked dry. He writhed and struggled frantically. But he had no energy left. He was just a ghost in a shell.

Lowrie crawled through the muck. The pain had spread to his legs and he couldn't stand up. His heartbeat merged with the roar of the ocean. Something else was beating too. It was coming closer. It sounded blue. Just a metre more. Then he could die happy.

Elph watched it all helplessly. There was nothing he could do. That cretin was throwing it all away and he could only hover helplessly. The hologram had no physical powers … except visibility.

There was only one chance for the dark side. One hope, and it had to work. Elph buzzed to where Lowrie lay and adjusted his digital spectrometer. All it would take was one click and he would appear in the human wavelength. Elph extended all appendages, set his face to grimace, and flicked the switch.

Lowrie looked up. A small creature was floating before him. It was malignant, he was certain. Sinister gadgets were sprouting from his frame, and a green beam emanated from one eye. Lowrie's heart cranked up a notch. It was one notch too many. Shutdown!

They were linked, somehow. Because Meg felt Lowrie go.

'No!' she screamed, her remaining essence already fading.

Belch was leaving too, but he was going with a smile on his face. 'See you soon,' he laughed. 'Really soon.'

The tunnel opened above their heads, poking through the clouds like a straw in a giant cola. It sucked them up like a vacuum.

Meg stretched out to her partner; she called to him, but he couldn't hear her. His body was in the final stages of shutting down. Only the brain was alive, and not for very long.

Elph buzzed past her. 'Nice working with you,' he commented. 'Maybe we can play for the same team once I ditch the moron.'

Meg didn't even hear the words. She could only watch her tears fall on the only man who had ever cared for her. It was over, all over. And she had failed. Again.

Flit was crouched on the tunnel rim, as per his instructions. It sounded simple enough. One favour for Peter and he was in. No one must ever know. That was the condition.

He saw the whole thing. The cliff and the storm, and then that thing with the motorbike. Very exciting. This is what it must be like to have a television.

Then their essence ran out and the tunnel had them. Belch floated by, a line of drool hanging from his grinning lips.

'Nice day,' said Flit pleasantly.

'Arf,' responded Belch uncertainly.

Then came the girl. She wasn't looking his way, still connected to the ground. She would have to let go, or her soul would never find peace.

'Girly girl!' shouted Flit, the knight in shining armour.

Meg turned slowly, her face a puffy mask.

'Flit?' she said hesitantly.

'Yes, girly girl. Flitty Flit Flit. Girl remember stones?'

Meg frowned. 'Stones?'

'Yes. Girl not understand plain honest wordies? Stones. In pocket. Blue stones.'

Suddenly Meg did remember. The stones. Flit had given her two blue stones when they'd first met. Life stones. Extra batteries he'd called them. She hadn't understood at the time, but now ...

She fumbled in her pocket. They were still there. Blue and silver. Gleaming and hot. The second her fingers closed around them, her strength came back. The tunnel receded, its pulse weakening in her veins. And Meg floated back down to the supine old men.

It was a terrible thing to think, but Lowrie looked pathetic. The rain had destroyed all his new gear, and there was a stream of mud flowing over his cheek. He wasn't breathing. But there was still a spark. An orange spark behind his right eyeball.

Meg placed one of the stones on his forehead, and it sank like ice into a hotplate. The effect was instantaneous. Lowrie's eyes shot open and he drew in the desperate breath of a sponge diver.

'Meg?' he gasped through the rain. 'Am I ...'

'No,' replied his partner. 'You're alive. I don't know for how long. But alive anyway.'

Lowrie spat out a mouthful of mud and worms. 'What about those other ... things.'

'Gone, for good I think.'

'And you?'

Meg shrugged. 'I don't know. I have one of these stones. It should keep me here for a while. If you'd like that.'

Lowrie smiled a watery smile. 'Of course I'd like it. Who else would put up with all my moaning?'

That could have been it then. All settled, happy ever after. Except for Franco. He lay there catatonic. Not dead, but he'd never be truly alive again either. No one deserved that.

Meg caught Lowrie's eye. They both knew what had to be done.

'Goodbye,' said Lowrie simply.

'Bye,' mumbled Meg. She had to do it quickly, or she never would.

The stone sank into Franco's forehead, washing away the years. The life rushed back into his eyes. He was himself again, but not the same.

Meg took her stepfather's face in her hands. 'Did he show you what it was like?' she asked.

Franco nodded, the horror of hell still fresh in his mind.

'Good. Don't forget it.'

Her stepfather shook his head. He couldn't forget it, even if he wanted to. Things were going to change.

Of course, giving the stone to her abusive stepfather was an act of pure good. An explosion of soft white light picked Meg up and catapulted her gently into the mouth of the tunnel.

CHAPTER 14: HERE AND THEREAFTER

THE Atlantic Ocean rolled off towards America. Lowrie watched it go from the foot of a round tower. It was nice, still being around to appreciate nature.

He had more time now, he was certain of it. Meg had done something to him. Given him something. He didn't know what, but he was sure he wasn't going to waste it sitting in a flat feeling sorry for himself. He had Sissy Ward's number in his pocket, and a Visa card with a few bob still left on it.

A plucky sunray battered through the cloud cover and warmed his forehead.

'Thanks, partner,' he whispered at the sky, and spat over the Cliffs of Moher.

Meg was coming close to the fork. Up or down? The moment of truth. She squinted against the glow of hell's gate. Soot-blackened creatures were hanging on by their hooked toes, jabbing the unfortunate damned with vicious tridents. Meg held her breath, waiting for an invisible force to drag her down. It didn't come. She was floating straight

by. Meg allowed herself a relieved smile. Mam, she thought.
I'm on my way.

One of the winkle pickers launched himself into the
currents. It was Belch. He could never escape the infernal
gravity, but he might be able to reach just high enough …

Belch wrapped himself around Meg's torso. Insane
gibberings leaked from between his slobbering lips.

'Finn,' he muttered. 'Finn going down.'

That was it for Meg. She'd just about had it. After all this
time, he was still after her. A pit bull to the end. There was
only one thing to say.

'Belch,' she screamed, raising a booted foot. 'You can go
to hell!'

She brought the boot down squarely on his wet nose, and
the creature that had been Belch Brennan spiralled into the
flames, with Meg's name stretching behind him like a
prayer. Or a curse.

Damage-control time. Beelzebub wracked his brain for
a way to put a positive spin on the whole Finn debacle.
The Master had him waiting in the foyer. That wasn't
good.

A platinum-blonde Oscar-winner buzzed him in. 'The
Lord of Darkness will see you now.'

Beelzebub contemplated vaporizing her for suspected
casualness, but the Master was particular about his
secretaries. Some of them lasted a whole week before being
consigned to the scrap heap. Literally.

Satan was crouched in the corner of his office, playing a
Gameboy. 'Die, alien scum,' he was saying feverishly,
wiggling horny thumbs.

'Ahem,' said Beelzebub.

Satan froze. So did Beelzebub. Maybe ahemming the Master of the Underworld was a bit of a no no.

'You made me lose a life, Bub.'

'A thousand apologies, Master,' croaked hell's Number Two. 'I have important news.'

Lucifer rose from the marble floor. He was casual today. Sweatshirt and Air Satans.

'News about the Irish girl, I hope.'

Beelzebub swallowed. 'Yes, Master. News about the Irish girl.'

'Good news?'

'In the short term … no.'

The Devil looked up sharply.

'But in the long term, we've learned a valuable lesson.'

Satan raised an indulgent eyebrow. 'Which is?'

'Am … we've learned not to trust Myishi's holowhat-evers. One of them malfunctioned at a crucial moment and ruined the entire retrieval. We had the girl in the tunnel, for G– for Satan's sake.'

Lucifer clicked his talons on the desk. 'We had her in the tunnel, eh?'

'Red aura, the whole enchilada.'

Satan made a decision. 'That Myishi, too uppity by far. Put him in the sewage stream for a few centuries. We could do with a fresh filter.'

'Yes, Master,' bobbed Beelzebub, trying to hide a grin. 'At once, Master.'

He hurried to the door. Get out while the getting was good.

'Oh – and Bub?'

The demon tensed, expecting the excruciating agony of vaporization to strike him between the shoulder blades.

'Yes, Master?'

'There's a movie director due to arrive here today. Very gothic. Dark superhero stuff. I'm very interested to see what he can do with the decor around here. Meet him yourself. Personally.'

The Devil paused to crack every bone in his fingers.

'Don't foul it up this time, Bub. Or Myishi will have a companion in the sewage stream.'

Beelzebub bowed obsequiously. Always the theatrics, he thought. Always the theatrics.

'I don't know,' said Peter, tapping the screen of his brand new computer. (A programmer had actually made it to the Pearlies.)

'You have quite a record for a minor. Not a whole lot in the plus column.'

Meg had her 'I'm only a cute little girl' face on. It wasn't fooling anyone.

'Look here. Shoplifting. Fraud. Vandalism. Truant. I could go on, but the screen isn't big enough.'

'Use the cursor,' suggested Meg.

'I know about the cursor,' snapped Saint Peter, in a very unsaintly fashion. 'I'm trying to make a point here. You never know when to shut up, do you?'

'No,' said Meg, instead of shutting up.

'And you had to kick that Belch creature, didn't you? Violence in the tunnel. I think that's a first. Impressive, even for you.'

Meg mumbled something that she hoped sounded like an apology.

'Oh I don't know. I suppose you did give your stepfather the stone.'

Meg nodded. Afraid to speak.

'And you did help that mortal complete his Wish List.'

More nods, faster ones.

Peter stroked his beard a few more times. It was worse than waiting for your numbers on the lottery.

'Well, I suppose. OK, then.'

Peter reached beneath his desk and pressed a button. A door-shaped hole appeared in the sky.

'I know,' said Peter. 'It's not a pearly gate, but "pearly gate" looks better in print than "hole in sky".'

Meg kept on nodding – it seemed to be a winning formula.

Peter waved his finger at her and she began to float.

'Go on up,' he said gently. 'I think someone wants to see you.'

Meg Finn floated towards the hole in the sky. There was a figure in the doorway – she couldn't make it out yet, but she could smell the sweet scent of jasmine.